A HISTORY OF THE IMAGINATION

A HISTORY OF THE IMAGINATION

a novel
by NORMAN LOCK

FC2

NORMAL/TALLAHASSEE

Published by FC2 with support provided by Florida State University, the
Publications Unit of the Department of English at Illinois State Univer-
sity, the Illinois Arts Council, and the Florida Arts Council of the Florida
Division of Cultural Affairs

Address all inquiries to: Fiction Collective Two, Florida State University,
c/o English Department, Tallahassee, FL 32306-1580

ISBN: Paper, 1-57366-115-5

Library of Congress Cataloging-in-Publication Data
Lock, Norman, 1950-
  History of the imagination : a novel / by Norman Lock.— 1st ed.
    p. cm.
  ISBN 1-57366-115-5
  1. Safaris—Fiction. 2. Africa—Fiction. I. Title.
  PS3562.O218H57 2004
  813'.6—dc22
                                        2004004922

Cover Design: Lou Robinson
Book Design: Tara Reeser

Produced and printed in the United States of America
Printed on recycled paper with soy ink

ACKNOWLEDGMENTS

5_Trope, The Absinthe Literary Review, Ambit, The Barcelona Review, Big Bridge, The Cafe Irreal, The Cream City Review, De Tijdlijn, Upstairs at Duroc, elimae, First Intensity, Friction Magazine, Idiom 23, Imago, The Iowa Review, Jejune, Linnaean Street, Literal Latté, The Literary Review, Mirata, NEeuropa Review, Nightsun, The North American Review, The Paris Review, Pig Iron Malt, Rampike, Seems, Stirring: A Literary Collection, The Southern Cross Review, StoryQuarterly, Lo Straniero, Sulphur River Literary Review, Tatlin's Tower, Unlikely Stories, Unsaid, Wascana Review

Acknowledged, also, is a debt to those who published various of the "histories," whose inclusion in this volume would have frustrated the novel's ultimate design: *Archipelago, The Brobdingnagian Times, Dirigible, Duct Tape Press, Lynx Eye, New Letters, Pangolin Papers, Paris/Atlantic, Tears in the Fence, Vowel Movement, Way Station Magazine,* and *The Woolly Mammoth.*

Sincere thanks is also given to the New Jersey State Council on the Arts, and to the publisher of Fiction Collective Two, R.M. Berry, and the press's able and amiable managing editor, Brenda Mills.

To my mother and father

For Helen Lock and Deron Bauman

And for Gordon Lish, with gratitude

CONTENTS

A Treatise on Desire   13

Caruso in Mombasa   25

Pavlova's Heels   35

The Sorrow of the Porters   41

A History of the Cinema   45

In the Time of the Comet   51

The Laughter of Women   61

The Scourge of Darkness   67

Growing Uncertainty   75

Raising Pennington   85

The City of Radiant Objects   93

Flight   99

Longing for Africa   105

The Anguish of Houdini   111

African Follies   117

The Aerodynamics of Dreams   123

The Book of Casualties   133

Hunting Icebergs   145

A Discourse on History 153

Extreme Cruelty 161

The Catalogue 165

Nervousness 171

The Geology of Love 177

A History of the Imagination 187

Opening New Territories 195

Dancing with the Invisible Man 205

Calling the Elephants 215

Beauty atones for the long death.
—Theodore Roosevelt, *African Game Trails*

A TREATISE ON DESIRE

Mrs. Willoughby woke, because of an insinuating pressure on her thigh. Hearing her stir on the other side of the thin wall that separated her room from mine, I went to her. "My sleep was disturbed," she said. "By someone who entered through the French windows without invitation and stood—there, at the foot of the bed. He stood a long time, watching me sleep, with his hand clutching my thigh. Don't ask me how I know."

"Perhaps you dreamt it," I suggested.

She lifted her nightdress so that I might regard five small bruises on an otherwise immaculate leg.

I regarded them gladly.

"One doesn't expect a nightmare mauling to leave marks!" she replied tartly.

"Was any further harm done you?" I asked, turning away to conceal my anxiety.

She was silent a moment, taking stock. Out in Kilindini Harbor, a hippo snorted. A hyena laughed somewhere in the night. She shook her head and sighed: "It is always so when Mr. Willoughby is out seeing to his affairs."

Mr. Willoughby managed the Uganda railroad. I considered placing my hand on Mrs. Willoughby's thigh in his absence, but didn't.

"And what of Lenin?" I asked instead.

She regarded her bruises, then said, "It's been ages since I've had him in my bed."

I cleared my throat meaningfully.

"Oh, Vlady is a very nice lover," she continued, "but too serious. He is death at a dinner party."

She sniffed the midnight air, delicately, through her finely shaped nose. I did, too, though mine is not nearly so handsome.

"There!" she said. "Underneath the gladiola—can you smell it?"

I smelled nothing.

"A pungency," she said, sniffing once more. "It is always so after I have been alone a while in bed: the pressure of a hand sufficient to wake me, the bruises, and a pungency underneath the gladiola."

In sympathy I put my hand on hers. In sympathy for her bruises the blood came out on my cheeks and my loins congested.

Heavy footsteps sounded on the veranda. I turned in time to see a shadow shamble into the topiary, to be swallowed by the greater darkness of a moonless night.

Mrs. Willoughby leaned over the marmalade dish.

"Will you stay the night with me?" she asked.

My heart jumped inside my safari jacket.

"Of course, delicious lady!"

"You misunderstand," she said in a tone of unmistakable reproof. "I want you to *watch*."

"Watch?"

(Was Lenin about to take up unlawful residence under Mrs. Willoughby's mosquito net once again while Mr. Willoughby tended to his railroad?)

"To see what visits me in the night."

My heart sank.

She dabbed my mustache with a napkin, to rid it of a crumb of toast. Her *eau d'cologne* lingered in the breathless Mombasa morning.

"Come; I want to show you something."

She took me lightly by the arm and guided me into the topiary. Beside the carefully clipped thornbushes taught to grow up outside her bedroom (ah, Beauty!), she pointed out the trampled grass and, in earth still impressionable after the recently ended rains, two enormous footprints that could only be characterized as simian.

I didn't know it at the time, but the footsteps trodden into the rain-sodden earth outside Mrs. Willoughby's bedroom had been left there by Prince Kong. (The same Kong who, as King, would ravish a jodhpured Fay Wray in the 1930s. In 1910, however, he was a moody young gorilla with as yet no appetite for virgin sacrifice.) He had left the family's hereditary stomping grounds in Central Africa and, after a long and circuitous peregrination, found himself in Mrs. Willoughby's topiary garden on the outskirts of Mombasa. At the time, many people were helplessly tramping the length and breadth of the continent, transfixed by the walking sickness, which then held sway. To my knowledge, however, no instances of animal contraction of the mysterious malady have ever been verified. Kong, as I would later discover, had been drawn to the open French windows by the strength of Mrs. Willoughby's desire.

August 1910

Mombasa

Dear Siggy,

An interesting case has lately fallen into my lap. A friend is being visited by an ape. She claims "it is always so" when she sleeps alone for any length of time. I would be interested in your analysis. Will you come?

Regards,
N.

September 1910

Zürich

Dear N.,

Visitation by apes is well-documented in the literature. The explanation lies in the unconscious, more precisely in the Id. Sexual deprivation is, quite obviously, at the root here. The ape is a figment of your friend's overactive imagination. (The ape appears frequently in medieval art as an emblem of licentiousness.)

I am detained in Zürich and suggest you take matters into your own hand. ("Fallen into my lap"—a revealing Freudian slip—indicates that you may have already done so.)

Yours truly,
Sigmund

P.S. Please do not call me "Siggy."

October 1910

Mombasa

Dear Siggy,

The ape is no figment! I can send you footprints to prove it!

Sincerely,

N.

October 1910

Zürich

N.:

You are clearly hysterical and delusional. Keep your footprints, and do not call me "Siggy"!!!

Sigmund Freud

I lay under Mrs. Willoughby's bed and waited. Up above me, Mrs. Willoughby slept, breathing in a way that reminded me of soft, fluttering things. Of moths, or a satin camisole dropped negligently over a chair, handled by a wind from an open sash. The jungle came a little way inside the room through the French windows thrown open to receive the balm of night. I listened to it register its agitations and alarms. Later, the moon rose above the topiary and threw the prickly shadow of the thornbushes onto the parquet, which was hard beneath my head.

Soon I, too, was sleeping.

I dreamt that Mrs. Willoughby was carried outside in the hairy arms of Kong (although I did not know his name at the time) into the moonlit topiary. There, on the wrought-iron garden bench, he made love to her.

"Sweet Mrs. Willoughby."

"What do you want, you big gorilla?"

"Deep in the Congo, I caught the night-bloom of your desire. I came here to stand by your bed and watch you sleep." He sighed. "I am smitten."

Then with ardor did Kong press Mrs. Willoughby to him. With ardor and with strength of arm. But she repulsed him.

"I'm not attracted to you physically."

He beat his breast.

"I can give you what no man can!"

(Leering braggadocio!)

"But I like men," she said.

"If you sleep with me, Beauty, there's every possibility that I might change into a man. I'm already a prince."

"I have a lover as well as a husband who, though seldom home, adds a certain *frisson* to my extramarital affairs."

Does she mean me? I wondered. Does she consider me her lover? We had twice or thrice dallied playfully under the mosquito net; but each time I had come away feeling that I had failed to measure up. Perhaps she means Lenin. Vladimir Ilich might not possess charm, such as one values in a dinner guest or pinochle partner, but he has charisma in spite of his unstylish clothes and muddy shoes.

"*Chérie*," said Kong, fiddling with Mrs. Willoughby's nightdress.

Mrs. Willoughby slapped the brute.

Kong wept, inconsolable.

I woke in Mrs. Willoughby's bed to find myself fiddling with her nightdress, with the buttons that did up the front. She was furious. "You have betrayed my trust!" she said. "You've played the brute as surely as that hairy ape did." I remarked that, unlike the hairy ape,

I had not bruised her; but she took no notice. "Leave me at once!" she commanded, giving me a shove. I fell out of bed.

"I was dreaming!" I protested in mitigation. "One isn't responsible for acts committed while asleep."

I sat in the library, admiring Mr. Willoughby's collection of Victorian erotica and a magnificent Cornwallis Harris portfolio of rhinoceros engravings. I also admired Mr. Willoughby's Bombay Gin; and my admiration, though not unbounded, was sufficient to drain the neck of a recently unstoppered bottle.

Mr. Willoughby's man knocked softly at the door before entering with a silver tray. He coughed discreetly into his fist, then, inclining towards me so that his black swallowtail opened gracefully, indicated a gilt-edged calling card.

I took the card from the tray and read: "Prince Ali Kong, the Congo."

"Shall I show the gentleman in?" Mr. Willoughby's man asked.

"I don't wish to see him," I said disdainfully.

"If you'll pardon me, sir—the gentleman insists."

"Tell Kong I am not at home!" I shouted. "Tell him that I do not talk to primates!"

"Very good, sir."

Mr. Willoughby's man nodded and left the library.

I folded my hands on the fumed oak desk (not in prayer, but in perplexity) and pondered the curious geometry in which I seemed to have become suddenly enmeshed.

And then, astonished, I looked towards the library casement: someone was outside, scratching at the window!

The following exchange occurred through the open window. To tell the truth, I was afraid to meet Kong otherwise. Gorillas, no matter how polished their manner, retain a dark and brutal instinct. Which is only natural. While Kong may have distinguished himself among beasts, he was one after all; his top hat, spats, gloves, and immaculate grooming did not for a moment make me forget his origins. While not one to lord it over the beasts, I nevertheless relish my superior evolution.

"You refused to see me," said Kong, offended.

"Yes."

"Why?"

"We can have nothing to say to each other."

I looked away, unable to meet his piercing gaze.

"I disagree," he said. "There's Mrs. Willoughby."

"What about Mrs. Willoughby?" I bristled, not liking her name in his mouth.

"It seems we are both in love with her," said Kong with admirable simplicity.

I disguised my admiration with a rebuke: "Whether I am or not is none of your concern! You, on the other hand, have no business loving her!"

Indignant, I began to close the window but was prevented by his large hand and muscular arm.

"Because we are of different races?" he demanded, and beneath the demand I detected the grievance of the perpetually slighted.

"Because we are of different species!" I snarled.

He kept silent a moment before continuing evenly: "Either you leave the field to me, or you will meet me on the field of honor."

Mrs. Willoughby was sleeping. I shook her—gently, then roughly—but she would not wake. Apparently, she had contracted the sleeping sickness, which, like the walking sickness, was then general throughout Africa. She might sleep for weeks—or months—

before waking. I undid her buttons and undressed her. I considered whether or not to make love to her while she slept but decided against it. To my mind it smacked of necrophilia—a practice I detested. I did, however, study her nakedness. It was pink and round and fragrant. It was the nakedness of a woman in the prime of life, and I longed to embrace it. But I continued in my resolve not to interfere with her sleeping.

I bit my lip and sighed, "Oh, Mrs. Willoughby!"

I prayed that she might wake, that I might gather her to me; but she did not wake.

I sat by the bed on a rattan chair and kept watch as I had promised her. Kong is here because she sleeps, I reasoned. He is no delusion or manifestation of hysteria, but a very real presence unleashed by Mrs. Willoughby's dreams. Neither nightmare nor incubus, but *substance* (even if hirsute). A pulse of erotic energy—embodied and clothed. Kong would be detained in Mombasa, in the vicinity of Mrs. Willoughby, who would be helpless before his depredations for as long as she slept. I had no faith in Kong's self-restraint or finer feelings, given the bruises imprinted on her thigh.

"Oh, wake up, Mrs. Willoughby!" I shouted. "Wake!"

She was far down in the depths of sleep. I would have needed a grappling hook to raise her.

Night fell and the shadow of the thorns invaded the room. A wind flooded through the French windows and with it a pungency underneath the scent of gladiola.

"I think you do not understand desire," said Kong.

I looked at the sleeping Mrs. Willoughby and assured him I did.

"I don't mean the sudden arousals of your kind that are just as suddenly quelled; I mean desire as a paroxysm of nature. Violent biological upheaval. Wildfire sweeping the blood. A glandular storm

wracking body and nerves. Savagery and exaltation unknown in
New York, London, or Paris."

He took off his hat and coat, spats and lemon-colored gloves,
his shirt and trousers. He stripped to his essence—the elemental condition of his kind. I saw strength of will revealed in a purely physical
nature—vitality that transcended brutishness. In spite of myself I
envied him. And then, just as quickly as he had divested himself of
the trappings of civilization, he put them on again.

"Where I come from," he said, "all is desire; all life comes into
being by its force; all is copulation and increase. All is—if you will
pardon me—the long, tireless fuck of creation."

Kong stroked the sleeping woman's thigh; she stirred in her sleep
and smiled.

"She knows," he said; "as long as she dreams, she knows desire's
force."

Fury rose up in me—fury that Mrs. Willoughby should be used
so. I pulled his hand roughly away.

He slapped my face with a lemon-colored glove.

"Cigars at dawn," he said.

Siggy, Siggy—how I wish you were here! To be challenged by an
ape in spats and yellow gloves to a duel with *cigars*! How absurd!
How Freudian! And how does one fight a duel with cigars?

We met in the summerhouse behind the topiary. We faced each
other across a pinochle table. Mr. Willoughby's man entered with a
mahogany humidor, which he placed on the green baize. On a distant lawn a badminton game was in progress. I listened to the shuttlecock strumming the racquets. Who can be playing badminton at
this hour? I wondered as Kong selected a cigar.

"Partagas," he said, sniffing it with the air of a connoisseur.

"One of Mr. Willoughby's favorites," his man said approvingly.

I chose a democratic Virginian with a Connecticut wrapper.

Mr. Willoughby's man clipped the ends in a miniature guillotine and, having returned them to us, lit them.

"Close the windows, then leave us," said Kong with a peremptory wave of his cigar's burning end.

The man left, shutting the door behind him.

We sat in silence, the heavy blue smoke tumbling in the light that fell through the closed summerhouse windows. Eyes watering, throat burning, I thought of Mrs. Willoughby asleep in her bedroom and wondered if she was worth it. Ashamed, I sucked vigorously at my cigar, expelling clouds of pungent smoke across the pinochle table. Kong was unperturbed.

The pungency! I said to myself. The pungency underneath the gladiola!

It was then I lost consciousness.

We seemed to make love under water. The air wavered, the light shook down over us. Mrs. Willoughby drifted, her long auburn hair floating like weed. I swam above her attentively, darting here and there to give her what pleasure I could. Had I spoken, I would have told her how I desired her; but I did not speak. Because of the water, because I had no wish to drown in the act of love, nor of speech either. I looked up at last and saw Kong, his broad face smiling in benediction. The end of his cigar extinguished.

I shrugged into consciousness in Mrs. Willoughby's bedroom. By what mysterious mode of locomotion I had arrived there, I cannot say. Mrs. Willoughby was gone. I examined the bed for signs of struggle but could find none.

I went out to the summerhouse in search of Kong; but he, too, seemed to have vanished without leaving so much as cigar ash to signify his presence. The gladiola were in full force, scenting the clear Mombasa morning. The shadows of the thornbushes were rolling back toward the topiary as the sun advanced. Bird song replaced that of the shuttlecock.

I found Mr. Willoughby's man in the conservatory, polishing the horn of the gramophone. Recordings of Brahms' four symphonies were stacked on a taboret. Mrs. Willoughby believed that plant life flourished in the presence of soothing melody. For this, she was derided as a crackpot. I had no opinion one way or the other, though I had often come to her defense in the Mombasa Hotel Bar, in order to insinuate myself into her favor.

"Have you seen Mrs. Willoughby?" I asked the man.

"Gone, sir," he replied, putting down his chamois cloth.

"Gone?"

"Carried off by the hairy gentleman."

It was as I had feared.

"Where?"

He pointed beyond the topiary to a darkness. An obscurity. A silence punctuated by strange cries.

"The jungle, sir."

He handed me a book bound in soft leather: *A Treatise on Desire* by A. Kong.

"He said I was to give you this."

I opened the book and began to read:

"*Desire begins in sleep…*"

CARUSO IN MOMBASA

Caruso stepped into the bright Mombasa morning. Sing to us, Enrico! we shouted. Sing "Pagliacci!" we cried. We were hungry for song—for melodies we could understand after so many years spent listening to tribal drums. To savage and inscrutable chanting. They were always there—the drumming, the chanting, the prayers to wooden gods—at the door of our minds and, after a time, in the vestibule, throbbing, insinuating their rhythms ever deeper until they seeped into our subconscious, subtly coloring it and (who knows?) changing us in ways we could not guess—altering the shape and chemistry of our brains. (I had lately begun to doubt the accuracy of

my observations, influenced as they must be by Africa!) For God's
sake, sing to us! we pleaded.

But he would not sing.

He turned from us and went back inside the hotel.

To hide. Because of his anxiety.

"His anxiety is different from yours," Freud explained as we
took our customary booth in the Mombasa Hotel Bar. "Yours is
acquired—the result of having lived too long in Africa."

I nodded.

He snipped the end of a cigar with a small instrument used in
lobotomies—souvenir of his days as a medical student at the University
of Vienna.

"Caruso's stems from the San Francisco Earthquake. It has traumatized
him."

The great tenor had been thrown violently from his bed in the
Palace Hotel during the cataclysm. It was not the sort of public demonstration
he had come to expect—even in the rough-and-tumble
American West.

Freud lit his cigar, studied its slow fire, then continued: "He carries
religious metals; but still he is frightened by the possibility of
disappearing, like Alice, down a hole in the ground."

Caruso had come to Mombasa in the hopes of recovering his
nerve.

"He needs a retuning," Freud joked, sending a cloud into the
room that made the twinkling siphon bottles above the bar grow
dim. "Africa is not the place."

Caruso had made the mistake of so many other great men I had
entertained in Africa: believing that, in the absence of civilization and
its discontents, he would find contentment. Rest. Serenity. But Africa
is not the place to convalesce. The hyperactive agents of imagination

and desire at work here, its ceaseless transformation, the feeling of claustrophobia that besets one in the wilderness, the bewildering diversity of forms—these are enough to agitate the most robust minds. Freud discovered, in Africa, captivating dementia and made them his constant study.

"An interesting case," he concluded. "I will take him on if he wishes." He opened his wallet and handed me his card. "Tell him to come see me on Thursday, at 10."

And then, after delicately separating the ash from the end of his cigar, he went to sleep.

I went to my room and listened to my Caruso recordings. I drew the curtains and sat in the dark to be alone with the Voice. From time to time I was moved almost to weeping—because of the beauty of the Voice and because of the memories that came flooding back: of Anna in the Hamptons, her dear face as it looked, looking out the window to the sea. I saw myself at her side, undoing the buttons of her blouse. I saw myself young and not yet undone by Africa. Why had I come here? Was it to wear a white linen suit and pith helmet and be called "*Bwana*"? Was it to lounge in the street with the Persian traders or be pulled about in a rickshaw by a sweating Sikh? Was it—as we declared over our gin and bitters in the Mombasa Hotel Bar—to settle the land with white, Christian men; to raise the natives out of savagery; and light the beacon of civilization in the heart of the Dark Continent? I lit the gas and looked at myself in the mirror: my face had a sickly, greenish cast. It must be the gaslight, I said to myself. I turned off the gas and opened the curtains. The tropic sun poured into the room. The shadows rolled back beneath the furniture, jumped up the walls, and shrank into the room's farthest corners. I put on my white linen jacket, my collar, and measured out a drink "in case." I saw myself in the mirror—a figure in a badly wrinkled suit, stained by drink, soiled by travel, singed here and there by my pipe's volcanic spew. No, I did not look well. I had drunk too much and worried too much and slept unsoundly for too long. At that moment I doubted myself and all men like me who come to Africa.

Sing to us, Enrico—sing! the people shouted from the windows and verandas of the pleasant houses of the pleasant town as Caruso walked its streets in search of who knows what balm. He went cautiously—not hugging the house fronts (afraid they might topple on him) nor keeping to the middle of the street (lest it open and swallow him), but along the very edge of the sidewalk.

"Won't you please sing to us, *Signor* Caruso?" begged the Mayor, who longed for the ornaments of European culture.

"Please, sir!" seconded the Chief of Police, who believed the mere sound of the Voice would quell the dark initiatives he sensed behind the expressionless faces of the natives.

But Caruso shook his head and, with ears cocked for overtures of tragedy, passed forlornly through the town.

Meeting Caruso outside his hotel, I gave him Freud's card.

"I cannot," he said, letting the card fall from his hand.

"Why not?" I asked.

"I do not wish to give up my secrets," he whispered.

"What secrets?"

"I cannot tell you. I cannot tell anyone."

He hung his head piteously.

"Freud is a doctor," I said brusquely, "and is forbidden to betray a patient's confidence."

Caruso shook his noble Neapolitan head (a head I could not believe harbored shameful secrets).

"I do not care to be hypnotized," he said shortly.

The Bishop stepped out of the sunlight in whose blinding noon-day glare he had been concealing himself.

"Freud does the devil's work!" he shouted.

I thumped the Bishop, knocking him down. His crosier clattered on the pavement. Ours was an ancient enmity, stemming from his denunciation of my "outrageous and insatiable lust," to which I responded with a sack of fresh elephant dung. He was alluding to my dalliance with Mrs. Willoughby, whose husband, Mr. Willoughby, was away, more often than not, managing the railroad. Neglected and unsatisfied, she had gone through a gang of lovers, most recent among them Vladimir Ilich Lenin, who had come to Africa to study colonialism.

Caruso helped the Bishop to his feet, smoothed his ecclesiastical skirts, and straightened his miter.

"It is wrong to abuse a priest," Caruso said with an exaggerated solemnity.

I whistled nonchalantly.

"Care for a sweet?" the Bishop asked as he took Caruso's hand and led him towards the bishopric.

"I am afraid to fall into a hole," said Caruso, trembling as they left the safety of the sidewalk.

The Bishop lifted a beringed finger into the air and intoned: "It is better to fall into a hole in the ground and be crushed upon the rocks than to fall into error and lose all hope of eternity."

(Oh, how I should love to kill him!)

"I doubt it!" cried Caruso as he broke away from the Bishop and raced pell-mell for the harbor.

Caruso sat in a native dhow, at anchor, a little way from shore.

I swam to him through the blue water, heedless of what might lie hidden at the weedy bottom: the shark, the barracuda, the crab.

"What do you want?" he asked.

"To help you," I replied, clambering wetly aboard the narrow boat.

"Careful, you'll scuttle us!" he shouted. And then, throwing his arms wide in an histrionic embrace of the invisible, he said, "The world is fractured, and through the seams they come for me—for Caruso!"

Melodrama may be fine on stage, but in life it is contemptible. Much annoyed, I shook him—"in order to bring him to his senses," I later told Freud, who frowned at my unscientific approach to the treatment of hysteria.

"Why should you wish to help me?" Caruso asked.

"I adore you," I said, stroking his boot ingratiatingly. "Your voice."

"I've lost it," he lamented.

"Because of your anxiety."

"Because of my fear," he said.

"Because of the earthquake."

"Yes," he admitted, much ashamed. "Fear is unbecoming in a man."

I urged him to talk to Freud—the Talking Cure—wonderfully efficacious—miraculous even!—his office on Queen Victoria Street an island of calm—the furnishings tasteful—the light behind the blinds dim and restful—the couch so very comfortable! One is soon lost in a labyrinth of cigar smoke.

"I'm in therapy myself," I told him, lying down on the bottom of the boat. "For my anxiety, which is considerable; for my dreams, which are lurid and unsettling. I assure you, I have been helped! I have slept soundly on that couch!"

"I intend to sleep here," he answered. "On the dhow."

"Won't you be uncomfortable?" I asked, studying the sky for portents.

"I can't sleep on land anymore," he mourned.

"Aren't you afraid of drowning?"

He looked into the distance—at the edge of the bay breeze-blackened and trimmed in white sails, where the sea enters the harbor and the sky, disentangled of hills and houses, soars.

"The ocean is beautiful," he said shyly so that I sat up to regard him.

"Yes, Enrico, it is beautiful," I agreed.

"A long thread runs through the water from Naples to Mombasa—to this dhow. See?" He dipped his hand into the water, and I seemed to see a thread; but it may have been a trick of sunlight on the tilting bay. "From the Tyrrhenian Sea to the Mediterranean to the Indian Ocean—a thread."

We were silent for a time, watching the white steamships unravel in the distance. The white sails. The clouds.

I held his hand for friendship's sake.

"It is my nerve," he said, "which was lost."

"And now will you sing, Enrico?"

He shook his head wistfully. His anxiety may have slept in the ocean's wet folds, but he knew that he must return to land where the thread would break and the sky tangle in the trees and houses on the hill.

"I will hum for you," he said. "'*Ch'ella mi creda libero.*'"

Let her believe that I have gained my freedom.

Roosevelt put up at the Mombasa Hotel with his son Kermit. They had come to Africa to forget the election—"my abdication," T. R. called it. They would hunt the big game species. They would study the flora and fauna of Africa. They would "rattle about the bully bush" and live the life of a man—and "to hell with politics and the Wall Street crooks!"

"May I see your *Times*?" I asked Teddy as he laid his newspaper on the bar and prepared to leave.

"Help yourself," he said. "Though I warn you: the news is all bad."

He glanced at Freud, who had joined me for an afternoon cocktail.

"May I introduce my friend, Dr. Sigmund Freud? Sigmund, this is Theodore Roosevelt, former President of the United States."

Teddy nodded warily; Freud nodded warily in return. They gazed at each other a long moment, taking each other's measure.

"I do not approve of you, sir," Teddy said finally. "Hysteria's nonsense—women's nonsense! A strenuous, outdoor life will soon drive the vapors from your patients' heads."

"Balls," Freud replied.

Teddy's mustache bristled.

"I will see you again, sir!" he sniffed.

(He would, too—in therapy, in Freud's Queen Victoria Street practice after Teddy's nervous collapse in the wilderness.)

Freud sat in wounded silence while I rattled about in the newspaper.

"Look!" I said, pointing to a picture in astonishment. "Caruso! In the *Times*!"

Freud looked.

"It's a review of his performance in *Fanciulla del West* on December 10th at the Metropolitan!"

I put the paper down in perplexity.

"So?" said Freud.

"He was in Mombasa on December 10th! That was the day I thumped the Bishop."

Freud took off his spectacles, fingered the bridge of his nose, put his spectacles back on.

"His body may have been in New York, but his mind was in Mombasa," he said.

I didn't understand.

"The mind wanders," he said, "and, more often than not, it wanders to Africa—the shimmering image, the emblem of desire. Africa of the green hills and the lion...the hippos among pink and purple lilies...the endless strings of flamingos above the river."

"And women whose skin is the color of night," I added, my voice thickening.

Freud nodded.

"For every man, a different Africa," he said.

"So Caruso is not here?"

"Here and not here..."

He fell silent while he studied the coffee grounds at the bottom of his cup.

"And you?" I asked.

"I'll know for sure when I've finished my self-analysis. But I suspect I'm in Vienna, having coffee and pastries with someone far more alluring than you."

"And me?" I asked doubtfully.

"In the Hamptons with your Anna, perhaps."

(But I had fled that life, or so I believed.)

Suddenly desperate, I jabbed my leg with a fork and yelped.

"A dream of pain," he sighed.

I went to the harbor to see Caruso. Tied up to the dock, the dhow was empty.

"If you're looking for that Italian, he's not here," a dockhand said.

He was leaning against a bollard, smoking his pipe in the quickly falling dark.

"Where did he go?"

"He went with the Moroccan pirates," he replied, knocking the dottle into the bay.

I sat in my room and listened to my Caruso recordings. Where are you, Enrico? I asked. On the beautiful ocean following your thread away from the terror of annihilation—out into the Indian Ocean, then on, to the Mediterranean and Tyrrhenian Seas—to Napoli where once you sang with insouciance and no thought of art? Are you singing to the Moroccan pirates in gratitude? Is it for them you have been saving your voice? Will they use you, like a siren, to lure innocent ships into the mist where they will board them with drawn swords? Or have you already charmed the pirates into civility?

I turned off the gramophone and went out into the town, onto the empty, dark streets. Through the windows of the houses I saw women dressed in light, moving dreamily toward unseen rooms, following the taut thread of desire.

Anna, I ought not to have let you go in Kampala after the lion had surprised you among the wild olive trees!

I began to run, frightened by the sudden emptiness that loomed just beyond the rings of gaslight. I felt the old anxiety returning. The nervousness.

Sigmund! I shouted, and the stillness shattered like glass. Sigmund! I shouted all the way down Queen Victoria Street, to Freud's office, where I hammered on the door till the askari policemen dragged me away.

PAVLOVA'S HEELS

Our energies waned and with them our belief in the enterprise. The Beacon of Civilization, which we had dragged behind us all those many years in the wilderness, was all but extinguished.

The Bishop was summoned. He arrived, dressed in full canonicals, with the might and majesty of the church upon him. We scurried out of the way so as not to be crushed.

"We want to go back," we said. "We are worn out with our ceaseless comings and goings."

We showed him the state of our boots, the holes in our trousers, our frayed cuffs. We showed him our untended cheeks and chins as proof of our growing indifference.

The Bishop thundered like a thousand kneeling benches let down at once on a stone floor. His crosier flashed with anger and prerogative.

We were not impressed.

"Let us pray," he said, nodding into the wings for the mission boy to bring on the purple cushion. The cushion that was tasseled with gold.

"No!" we shouted, lifting our voices in revolt.

We stamped our feet and whistled. We sent a deputation. We distributed provocative pamphlets. Several of my colleagues (I blush even now to think of it!) shied bustard eggs at the Bishop's miter.

He cursed us soundly one and all and, picking up his skirts, made haste to leave. The suddenness of his departure raised a cloud of swirling dust, brightened here and there by crimson petals felled in the reckless sweep of his crosier.

"The Bishop's Departure," as it would come to be called, was a seismic event without precedent in that part of the world.

What to do? we asked ourselves. What to do?

It was then that Georges Méliès surprised us by appearing out of nowhere. He did so with the celerity of a shaft of light through a hole in a cloud.

"Why should you be surprised?" he asked. "I was a magician before I began making films."

We asked him what he wanted on the Dark Continent.

"To make an African Fantasy," he answered. "Will you guide me into the jungle? Will your porters carry my camera, lighting instruments, and props?"

We conferred. Quigley praised the filmmaker's *The Trip to the Moon*, which he had seen in 1902. Quigley never missed an opportunity to show off his cultural superiority. We denounced him among ourselves as a prig.

Hanby proposed we ditch Civilization's Beacon and make mov-
ies.

"Seeing as how we have nothing better to do."

I had no opinion one way or the other.

Captain Slade, however, made a pointed observation: "There
have been precious few women in these pages!"

I was about to mention Mrs. Willoughby when Mlle. Pavlova
knocked.

"Hello," she said. "I've come to Africa to collect native dances.
Do you know where I can find any?"

We forgot all about Méliès, I can tell you that!

We offered Pavlova some boiled bongo, which she ate with relish. During the ritual Smoking of Cigars, she regaled us with anec-
dotes of her recent tour of Japan. All agreed she was a most amusing
dinner guest.

To help finance her newest expedition (how different from ours!),
she had accepted a commission from O'Sullivan's Heels for an African testimonial. She gave me a handbill printed with an earlier en-
dorsement, which I faithfully reproduce here:

Mlle. Pavlova, the Incomparable says:

"It is with pleasure that I state to you that O'Sullivan's
Heels of new live rubber give me great comfort in walking. I have them on all my walking shoes and also on a
number of my dancing shoes. I recommend them to every member of my company."

O'Sullivan's Heels are worn by successful people everywhere.

I wondered if the Bishop wore them under his skirts. He had
exited with a liveliness in his step which belied the weight of his
authority.

Pavlova showed us her O'Sullivanized boots. Her pale calves aroused us instantly.

"Dance for us, Pavlova!" we begged. "Kick up your O'Sullivan's Heels! Perhaps then we shall feel the joy of life return!"

"But, gentlemen—where?" she asked, looking around her at the entirely too realistic scenery. "I must have structure! I must have a suitable venue!"

Stephens remembered having seen an ornate proscenium arch hidden in a bamboo grove. We adjourned there. On the way, we passed Méliès, who withdrew discreetly behind a tree.

"Your turn will come!" we promised him in our gratitude.

Pavlova reprised her famous roles in *Giselle*, *Swan Lake*, *Les Sylphides*, *Don Quixote*, and *Coppélia*. We were, to a man, captivated. Quigley requested the *Dying Swan* solo dance Michel Fokine had created for her in 1905—and which he, Quigley, had seen "in Paris." Disgusted, we pelted him with elephant dung.

Night fell. We lit colorful Japanese lanterns and hung them in the trees. Each of us took his turn dancing with Pavlova. Our hearts opened. In return we offered to show her a native dance.

We crossed the harbor of Kilindini in a dhow and walked two days south to a Nyika village where a funeral dance was in progress. The countryside was hilly, the ground stony; but Pavlova took it in stride in her O'Sullivan's Heels.

"Like a trooper!" said Captain Slade, who was by now smitten.

The Nyika dancers wore queer little wickerwork baskets tied to their legs. Dry beans rattled inside as they moved.

"This death dance has more life and go in it than any dance I've seen," declared Pavlova admiringly.

We spent the night under a baobab tree, overlooking the Indian Ocean. In the small hours, Captain Slade crept out of his tent.

Pavlova left early with the funeral dance, mapped out on a sheet of butcher paper, and a basket of beans.

"Goodbye," she said.

Captain Slade entered a period of misery.

"Is there anything I can do for you?" I asked him one night at the Mombasa Hotel Bar.

"Dance for me!" he answered drunkenly. "Dance as Pavlova did!"

I assure you I did not disappoint him.

THE SORROW OF THE PORTERS

The porters were weeping. They could not go on. They put down their burdens. They went into the papyrus grove to be alone with their sorrow. Their tears mingled with the river and turned the dry elephant paths to mud. We were stunned by this show of dejection from the ordinarily cheerful porters. They sometimes suffered greatly from exhaustion, hunger, and thirst; but safari life is, for the most part, pleasant and picturesque.

We conferred among ourselves, wanting to understand. They bore upon their black backs the entire enterprise. And with it our hopes. But that was not the only reason for our concern: we liked them.

They were good-hearted and amusing fellows. Of course like all savages and most children they had their limitations, and in dealing with them firmness is even more necessary than kindness. Not that we were unkind. We were not. We fed them well; we gave them suitable clothes and small tents. All in all, safari life is a great advantage to them.

"Surely they can see that!" we said, ashamed of the resentment which, in spite of ourselves, was stealing over our hearts.

"Perhaps we should try and cheer them up," suggested Hanby.

"Put on a show!" proposed Carlson.

"We'll soon bring them out of their dumps!" laughed Captain Slade.

We knocked together a little stage. We had a Rhodes piano and some elementary lighting instruments. For scenery we had Africa.

"I have never played before a weeping house," said Quigley, who went in for amateur theatricals.

(In my mind's eye I saw a house weeping from its windows.)

"Proceed," said Carlson, taking it upon himself to stage-manage the production.

We pummeled the porters with persiflage and tickled them with feathers. We performed the Savoy Operas in Swahili and bombarded them with badinage. We impersonated cabinet ministers and behaved like perfect idiots. At our wits' end, we wiggled, whooped, and wallowed. And then, throwing away the last remaining shreds of our dignity, we did our silliest walks. To no avail. Nothing we did could stem the tide of their weeping. Exhausted, they lay down at last and slept; but still the tears seeped through their closed eyes. Oh, it was pitiful to see!

"Perhaps it is the absence of women," said Captain Slade, who still carried a torch for Mlle. Pavlova.

"Perhaps the moon is having an effect," said Quigley.

"Perhaps we should ask them," said Blunt, who was as his name suggests.

We woke Muhammad and Bakari, two excellent men, loyal and enduring.

"What is your sorrow?" we asked them.

The fault, it turned out, was mine.

"We have been too long on the margins of your story," they said. "Scarcely a day goes by in which we do not play a part, but we are like the papyrus grove or the Kitanga hills or the red lizards—mere exotic decoration. We hardly know ourselves anymore! It is for this we weep. This is our sorrow."

Kassitura woke and rebuked me, "It is always the same when you speak of me: 'Kassitura played his harp.' I assure you I am much more than that!"

Ali, a particularly faithful and efficient porter, woke next.

"You seem to think it quaint that we should be fond of umbrellas," he chided. "Do we laugh at your ridiculous jodhpurs and hats?"

"I don't like this," I confided to Pennington.

"Shall I shoot the whinging bastards?" he asked.

I shrugged, refusing to commit myself.

Then the Bishop arrived, complaining of vilification.

"You won't get away with your libels!" he threatened, shaking his crosier at me. "I am not a man to be mocked with impunity."

"Shall I shoot *him*?" Pennington asked, keen to use his Holland.

"Not yet," I said.

At that moment, the news reached us that a hyena had seized Major R. T. Coryndon, administrator of Northwestern Rhodesia, and dragged him out of bed. I was thankful for the diversion.

The porters resumed their weeping.

Dance music drifted through the trees.

Georges Méliès appeared. We had promised him the use of the porters for his filming of an African Fantasy, but this was not the time.

"We're sorry," we said.

Disappointed, he left without a word.

"We will do it yet!" I shouted after him.

Lord Renshaw crossed the stage from left to right. I waited for him to return, but he didn't. Perhaps he sensed I wanted to borrow money.

The Bishop tripped over a tent peg and could not get up because of the weight of his vestments.

The porters were forgotten.

We went to the dining-tent for a game of hearts. In the morning the porters would rise and take up their burdens. If not, we would hire others. There are many men in Africa who would love to wear the blue blouse of a porter. Who would love to accompany us into the dark heart of the continent.

That night Pennington had his throat slit.

A HISTORY OF THE CINEMA

Now, Méliès.

I was gnawed by the tooth of remorse for putting him off so long. He dogged me for days—unobtrusively, as only a magician can who chooses not to be seen. With his effects hidden most likely under his high silk hat, he crept behind me through the bush.

My heart began to misgive me in Entebbe. I stopped and turned in time to see him slip beyond my sight lines. A glimpse of black sleeve with a trick or two up it, a colored scarf, an egg—a fleeting glimpse was all I had before he disappeared. He was a virtuoso of legerdemain—grant him that—the toast of Parisian variety before taking up the cinema after the success of the Lumières. I would not hesitate even now to climb into the sword cabinet under his direction.

"Now, Méliès!" I shouted, throwing my voice into the jungle so that he'd know that I, too, am capable of theatrical illusion.

Out he came.

The landscape no longer pleased us, nor the myriad of colorful birds. Why, I could not say unless satiety had accomplished what the seroot, with its vicious bite, and the sleeping-sickness fly could not: turned us away. We could not leave; our return ticket was contingent upon the fulfillment of our commission. But we could decorate the interior with hand-painted undersea plants, jeweled fish, and gold stars pasted to the black dome of unconsciousness. Méliès, with his cinema of enchantment, was just what we needed. We drank powerful herbal infusions and dreamt.

"Is it heavy?" I asked Ali, the porter, who had a piece of Méliès' cinema apparatus on his back.

"No, it weighs nothing at all," he said. "It is a feather—it weighs no more than a dream."

And so did they all say, each in his blue porter's blouse moving through the liquid night. For it was night, of course, in which we moved—night with its sweet airs, its moon and stars, and with the strange cries of birds. Later, the stars would sift down onto the lawn, the moon catch in the high branches of a thorn tree while the song of the night birds dropped like stones into the silence.

"My God," I said, "I had no idea it was beautiful!"

"It isn't," said Méliès, adjusting his camera lens to admit the light from an instrument. "It is my art that makes it so."

And the infusions.

And our terrible need.

And the many delicate motors humming all about us, which may be the sound of our autonomic systems.

"Light the gas," said Méliès.

We did, and the blue flames jumped up into the night.

"Softer," said Méliès.

We turned the jets down and the night flooded back, a black Nile.

Ross caught the walking sickness and set off at a brisk pace towards the equator.

"Ross!" we called, knowing full well there was nothing we could do to stop him.

"If Louis and Auguste were here, they would make a film of his walking," said Méliès. "I, however, prefer something more meaningful."

He was referring to the Lumières, who with their *cinématographe* captured movement for its own sake.

"Méliès enjoys the narrative possibilities contained in movement," asserted Quigley, who had seen the filmmaker's *Cinderella* in 1900 and, two years later, his charming fantasy *The Trip to the Moon.*

"But the Lumière brothers take as their subject the ordinary *femme* and *homme*!" cried Dr. Landis, a naturalist from the Smithsonian whose aversion to unlicensed imagination was well known even in Africa.

He was unhappy with our "escapism," not to mention our use of native pharmaceuticals. He struck a solemn pose and unstoppered himself: "Are we to have a cinema of childish fancy or one of social engagement?" He adjusted his pose for the camera. "Are we to abandon the hard-won realism of Zola and Ibsen for the *commedia dell'arte*?" he thundered so that the night birds grew silent.

"Social responsibility is all well and good," replied Hanby, who had none. "But I go to the theater, when I go to the theater, to take in a little stage *dishabille* and have a good laugh."

"You are an ignorant man," said Dr. Landis, growing taller and taller in his high dudgeon.

"That is precisely the reply I would expect from a man who wears his socks to bed."

The two of them would have begun to brawl had not a timely procession of giraffes paraded by, their long necks swaying indolently.

"Enchanting!" Méliès said as he cranked his camera. "This is just the thing I'm looking for! Where can I find more?"

I proposed the banks of the Guaso Nyero on the edge of a mimosa grove.

The Guaso Nyero runs along the equator eastward into the dismal Lorian Swamp. At our camp it was a broad, muddy stream infested with crocodiles.

"You will like the crocodiles," I promised Méliès. "Crocodiles in the moonlight are splendid."

The moonlight changed the landscape into legend, the same landscape which we had recently come to loathe. We stared in rapt fascination at the crocodiles whose backs wore silver scales. They drifted down the river or stirred in the mud, dreaming saurian dreams.

Perhaps I should mention here that we had entered a time neither geologic nor historic. It was not quite the Dream Time of the Australian Aborigines either, but it did emit stirring semi-quavers that entranced us.

Méliès was ecstatic. The film clattered in his camera. The porters shifted scenery or operated lighting instruments to "enhance the effect." I wound the gramophone: a serenade for strings enhanced the silence. Reconciled, Hanby and Dr. Landis danced in the intricate shadows of the mimosa trees.

"I crave the suspension of your disbelief," said Méliès; and we suspended it, willingly.

The gas jets bloomed.

The crocodiles slipped through the water like silver daggers.

The porters enhanced.

I wound the gramophone.

Hanby and Dr. Landis went into the mimosas to be alone.

Just then Halley's comet fizzed across the black, black night.

"What an effect!" we shouted.

Méliès bowed.

Our applause was extreme, our admiration unbounded. Were we wrong to love him?

"The film will be a triumph," he said with a simplicity most becoming in a man of genius.

Ross returned from the equator, tears streaming from his eyes.

"Thank you!" he called. "Thank you, my friends, for this dream!"

Yes, I would have climbed into the sword cabinet gladly and—should the trick misfire and I be pierced to the quick—I would have smiled.

Smiled!

We kept watch through the luminous hours, refusing sleep and all infusions. No rhino appeared, nor did any harm befall us. By first light the old affection for Africa had returned—such was our pleasure, such was our joy.

Were we wrong to love him when all around us wild beasts waited to spring with their sharp teeth?

IN THE TIME OF THE COMET

Each night when the tropic sun abruptly ceased (to resume or not), we began to be afraid, because of the comet blooming in the sudden dark. "The velvet dark," purred Quigley. Although a metaphysician and *habitué* of Miss Stein's on the rue de Fleurus, his tropes were commonplace. Remarking on the comet and other portents, Freud had prophesied that ours would be an anxious century. And we *were* anxious each evening when the nightjars invaded the sky and the darkness (velvet or not!) scythed about us dangerously. We would hurry then to a place of refuge—in my case the Mombasa Hotel Bar or (unable to avail myself of the consolations of Mrs.

Willoughby) the brothel.

"It is *fin de siècle* man's dread of female sexuality and its homicidal power that makes us anxious," said Sigmund, rummaging in
the *cocotte's* closet for her shoes. He was investigating fetishism at
the time. I objected that the century had already turned, ten years
earlier. "In fact but not in the mind," he replied. "In the mind, these
things linger on." And aren't women also anxious? I wanted to know.
"Women," he whispered so as not to be heard by one lying beside
me, "are not like you and me."

"Would you like a nightcap?" the madam asked.

"Yes," I said gratefully, feeling the old thirst rise up in me once
again.

I took my drink into the library where several gentlemen were
examining leather-bound volumes of erotic illustration. I finished
my drink and smoked a cigar, a Dannemann Pierrot. It was then I
noticed Gregg, busily writing at the madam's secretary desk.

I peered rudely over his shoulder.

"Turkish?" I asked.

"Pardon me?" he said, looking up from his notebook.

"Is that Turkish you're writing, or perhaps Persian?"

He snickered.

I twisted his arm painfully. He was of slight build, and I had no
doubt that I could subdue him.

"Why do you snicker?" I demanded.

"At your evident ignorance of orthographies."

Having failed to daunt him, I let go his arm.

"Please accept my apologies," I said obsequiously. I was curious
to know the meaning of his strange marks.

He closed his book, eyeing me with disdain.

"Care for a drink?" I asked.

He didn't drink.

Or smoke cigars.

Nor—he assured me—did he dally.

"Not with women of ill repute!"

"Then what are you doing in a house of ill repute?" I inquired.

He took me by the arm and led me onto the balcony.

"There is no better view of the night sky than this!" he nearly shouted in his excitement.

I looked nonplused.

"To see the comet!"

Henri Matisse barged in with canvas and easel.

"I was told there was an *odalisque*?" he said, looking around the library.

"There are no *odalisques* in Mombasa," said Gregg with obvious relish.

Matisse bowed his head in disappointment.

"I was promised!" he pouted. "I've come all the way from the Cote d'Azure to paint an *odalisque*!"

(Oh, he was annoyed!)

"There are *cocottes*," observed one of the perusing gentlemen; "and courtesans and other women of the night."

"The *night*!" Gregg sighed, for night interested him profoundly.

"Do they dress in *culottes*?" Matisse asked, hope kindling in his eyes.

"I'm afraid not."

Hope extinguished in an instant, and with it the light.

"I know an *odalisque* in Morocco," I said, wanting to help.

"Morocco is far," Matisse said wearily; "and I have already come such a long way!"

He unstrapped his easel and set it down. I noted a freshly sized canvas waiting for its *odalisque*.

"There is, however, a comet..." said Gregg, who was obsessed with (as I would later hear him call it) "the poetry of night."

"Rooms are what interest me," Matisse replied airily. "Rooms and women who lightly move in them."

"But the comet appears only once in seventy-six years!" Gregg asserted.

"Perfect pleasure is rarer still," said Matisse.

"The comet! The comet!" shouted Gregg from the brothel balcony.

I pulled the sheet over my head.

"Not now, John!" I moaned.

He climbed into bed with us—with me and a comely young woman who may have lacked harem pants but was, in my opinion, every bit as nice as any *odalisque*.

"But it's beautiful!" he cried. "Heavenly tracery...vestige of the hand that sketched the universe...the shining thought of the Creator...the—" He expatiated on the comet.

(Is it the comet one sees or its imprint, its incandescent present or fiery past? Interesting questions; but the woman lying next to me in humid, unclothed expectancy was far more interesting.)

"We are afraid of the comet, John," I explained patiently. "All Mombasa is afraid."

"Nonsense!"

"Even Sigmund is afraid of what it harbingers for the world."

(The Age of Dread.)

"The comet is an expression of universal constancy," Gregg declared. "A promise of eternal return."

(Many would say catastrophe.)

"Make him go away!" the woman cried.

(The bed was meant for two!)

Matisse entered, redolent of oil paint.

"What is going on?" he asked, getting into bed with us—with me, Gregg, and the woman who was now fit to be tied.

Sensing this, Matisse quickly tied her to the bed posts with sash cord.

"I wish to paint you by comet light," he told her.

Gregg looked on approvingly.

The woman protested noisily; the madam entered, followed by a stranger with tripod and camera.

"What is going on?" she asked while the photographer set up his equipment.

"Art," Matisse replied simply.

"Painting is finished," the photographer sneered. "Photography is the only art suitable to the twentieth century."

Insulted, Matisse threw down his brush.

"Untie me!" the woman demanded.

"No!" shouted the painter.

"Yes!" shouted the photographer, whose specialty was motion.

Scissors appeared suddenly in the madam's hands. I watched spellbound as comet light played along its blades.

Sigmund stepped out of the closet where he had been lucubrating.

"Castrator!" he screamed. "Vampire!"

The madam cut the cord.

"It is the fault of the comet," she said indulgently. "The comet makes everyone nervous."

"Muybridge is an enemy of art," Matisse complained. (Muybridge was dead—but what did Africa care?)

We were walking the streets of Mombasa in search of local color.

"His photographs are academic studies of motion without emotion. Their purpose is not pleasure, but efficiency."

Having no opinion, I said nothing.

"Aren't you at all concerned about the future of art?"

"No," I answered truthfully.

We stopped at the entrance to an alley. Teddy Roosevelt leaned against a wall, embittered by exile. The sun flashed angrily on his wire-rims.

"I would not go in there," he warned.

"Why T. R.?"

"One does not easily return," he said.

(Was it the alley he meant, or history in whose maze he now thought himself hopelessly lost?)

I looked into the alley. There was nothing unusual: beggars and old men. Women squatting in the shadows. Broken crockery. The pungent smells of cooking and unwashed bodies. The rattle of cans and that shrill music that seems a red string winding sinuously through the meager, dusty trees.

At one point I seemed to see Anna, who had left me in Kampala because of the lion.

"Anna!" I shouted.

The sun shattered in a pane of glass, and I saw her no more.

My mind went elsewhere.

To the dead sparrows at my feet.

To the cloud whose shape I very nearly recalled.

To the colorful geometry behind my closed eyes.

To the book I had picked up one afternoon in the Mombasa Hotel and read without comprehension as if entranced, my eyes catching on the barbs of its typography.

A boy appeared from out a doorway and said, "If you see Mr. Gregg, please tell him to come."

He was a ragged, dirty boy with a color suggesting illness.

"Come—come where?" I asked, my eyes stuck open in the way that sometimes happens in bright sunlight. "And for what reason?"

All sounds ceased.

The boy faded—swallowed up in sunlight or simply vanished in Africa where things come and go with a suddenness to make the head spin.

In the intense silence I heard Halley's comet fizzing in the darkness at the other side of the world.

"The comet drew me to Mombasa," said Gregg. "It seemed to say that here you'll find a subject fit at last for your shorthand. Here you will record the poetry of night instead of the dictation of businessmen. Look—"

He opened his book and showed me pages dense with a mysterious calligraphy, the spiked and loopy writing of dreams.

"Each night I trace the comet's path as it moves deeper and deeper into the mind."

"The mind?" I asked anxiously, fearing that all would once again prove illusory.

"The comet colors our dreams," he said. "Look—"

He pointed to the crest of a hill above the Indian Ocean where Marie Curie walked, her white nightdress glowing like a watch dial.

He pointed to Sousa marching over the waves, his sousaphone brimming with light.

He pointed to Einstein, whose eyes shone with luminous equations.

He pointed to Freud, cigar flaming in the darkness of Queen Victoria Street.

He pointed to the Wright brothers' fragile cage of light.

He pointed to the ragged boy in the alley, shining in his illness.

"Who is that boy?" I asked Gregg fearfully.

"He believes I can cure him; or, more precisely, the comet can and that I am its prophet." He smiled wryly. "It is what many in Mombasa believe."

I asked him if I was asleep and, if so, what light the comet shed on my dreams.

The light of desire, he said. The light of murder.

While Matisse slept and dreamed of painted *odalisques*, Eadweard Muybridge studied photographic plates. He had caught the comet's flight in a series of rapid exposures but was dissatisfied with the result.

"What happens *here* escapes me," he said, pointing to the blank space outside each frame, the border where one image ends and the next begins; "and that is what is most significant. The secret of the subject lies in what we cannot see."

"What happens beyond the margin is the poem," said Gregg.

"Is the *dream*," said Matisse from the depths of a voluptuous sleep.

I am asleep, or awake. Impossible to tell one from the other—in Africa during the time of the comet. Asleep or not, I am making love to a woman the color of night. The drapes are open wide to receive the comet's blessing, or curse. We move slowly among particles of light. A silver dust, they cling to our hair. Oblivious to us, Gregg sits by the window, taking the comet's dictation. Matisse sleeps; Muybridge sleeps, dreaming of horses and pugilists. Teddy Roosevelt looks at the sky and weeps.

Moved, I leave the woman and go to stand with him on the balcony.

"What is wrong, Mr. President?"

"No more," he says, "no more. It is Taft's turn at the helm."

"Your time will come again—your 'crowded hour.'"

"We are lost."

"We are in Mombasa," I say, taking his hand to comfort him.

"All of us will be lost in what comes."

He looks around him as if for his Rough Riders. At the hill, hoping perhaps to see San Juan Hill here beside the Indian Ocean. Looks at the woman asleep under the mosquito net—wanting Alice, his dead wife. Now he turns his eyes to the comet and shudders.

"I see in it the shape of death."

"It is only rock," I say. "Dust."

He shakes his head. He sees what I do not. The century unraveling from this single knot of light. He shakes his head at what he sees: war, ruin, death—all in this knot of light.

"The Age of Dread," says Freud, who is plumbing the depths of his dreams, in his room on Queen Victoria Street.

"No!" shouts Matisse, who has wakened. "There is something more. I can show you something more than death though there will be much of it in the twentieth century. Death will be ample."

"I suppose you mean art?" says Teddy cynically.

"I mean pleasure," Matisse replies.

But Teddy will have none of pleasure. He walks away without a look at the sleeping girl, who is naked and deserves a glance at least.

"And what is your opinion?" Matisse asks me.

As usual, I have none.

"You should take an interest in life!" he scolds.

Yes, Henri, but life terrifies me.

"What is it you do here in Africa?" he wants to know.

I shrug. I came out to hunt, to go on safari. But now...

"I drink gin and make love to women, when I may."

He approves of women and also of love.

"I miss the Cote d'Azure," he says wistfully.

"Then you should go home," I tell him. To your room overlooking the Mediterranean. To your paint. "At once, Henri!"

He picks up his easel, his night-blackened canvas, and steps into the darkness—disappears through a hole in the dark, or a door, though I do not hear it open or shut. Into a Fourth Dimensional Riviera, Quigley later claimed, where pleasure is heightened. (He had attended Povolowski's lectures in Paris on the Fourth Dimension and spent his free hours searching for it in Africa.)

I go inside. Gregg is at the window, transfixed by night's needle.

"How is it with you, John?" I ask.

He doesn't answer; apparently the poetry of night is wordless. He traces a hieroglyph in the air, signifying *comet*.

I think that he is crazy. I think we are all crazy and beyond Sigmund's curative powers. (I think Sigmund is crazy, too, but he amuses me.) I think that the comet is a flare sent up from a sinking world.

I lie down beside the woman. Asleep, she is floating under the mosquito net. I close my eyes and prepare for dreams of desire, or of murder. I pray the world will reassemble itself after the unconscious hours. I pray the century will not drown us.

THE LAUGHTER OF WOMEN

The delegation arrived to protest my "utter disregard of reality as it is commonly understood." I argued muscularly for my point of view, but they soon pinned me down. Waving a sheaf of soiled pages under my nose, they demanded immediate and unconditional redaction—"or else."

"Or else what?" I asked.

"We disavow all knowledge of you, repudiate any publications that may result from your present commission (though God knows who would be mad enough to publish such idiocies!), and, as final proof of our disdain—we cut off your legs."

"That last part seems a bit extreme," I said, ignoring the saw that was being sharpened for my rehabilitation.

"It will show the world you haven't a leg to stand on in these fantastic alterations of the truth."

"Define 'truth,'" I challenged, but they would not.

Instead, they set about to shake some sense into me. They did so until my back ached.

Growing tired or bored at last, they unpinned me from the ground. I rose, clapped the dust from my hands, and left for Mombasa without a word.

The steamer bumped against the dock in the picturesque harbor of Mombasa. White and wet with light, it was altogether worthy of the sea and our dreams of setting out upon it.

Standing on the shore, I thought: I shall buy a box of watercolors.

To paint the ship.

And the way the water wiggles.

And how the seabirds rise and fall.

(Underneath, surely there are exquisite fish!)

And look how the red-roofed houses climb the hill! I should like to go and visit the women in them.

But first I must see Raymond Roussel, who sits writing his own *Impressions d'Afrique* in his cabin.

"What year is it?" Roussel asked.

He was dressed for rain. I recall as well an opal ring, gray spats— what else? The loveliest fedora sitting on the bed.

"1910," I said.

"So early?" he sighed. "It will be a hundred years before they learn to read me."

I asked him why he didn't open the shutters. The light is wonderful in Mombasa! The harbor is among the most beautiful in the world! Fragrances arrive on the wind from the hill beyond—the perfume of heavy, purple flowers and of women who bathe in sandalwood and attar of roses.

"You are inventing again!" I heard the voice of the delegation say; but I closed my mind to it, so that it faded from my mind to be replaced by the laughter of women—women who are the color of coffee, of night, and also of pink erasers.

"Why don't you open the shutters?" I repeated because he had not bothered to answer me.

"So as not to be distracted," he replied irritably. "My work has nothing to do with *that*!"

"But your African impressions…" I began.

"Have nothing to do with Africa!" he snapped.

"With what then?"

"With words! Words to be dismembered, broken into pieces, and built up into something that 'has never been, which alone interests us.'"

He returned to his dismemberment.

The pen scratched.

I closed my eyes.

The ship swayed.

I dreamed of Anna.

And how they had beaten me.

"They beat me till my bones shook," I said, waking.

He gave me his chiropractor's card.

"He's your man."

"M. Roussel, I was hoping to stay with you, for a time. To rest. To absorb your genius. To take heart!"

"I can do nothing."

"But, *monsieur*—"

"I haven't room for protégés," he said, indicating with a wave of his hand the narrow cabin, the single bed.

"The world is all but unintelligible to me," I said anxiously.

"The world is governed by a secret grammar, which Roussel alone understands."

"What is it?" I nearly shouted in my passionate desire to know.

"It's a secret, I told you!"

He turned his back on me. The pen scratched some more.

"I like your hat," I said, to have something to say.

He lay on the bed then and talked about his hat. He had purchased it, he said, earlier that year while attending Minkowski's lecture on Space and Time to the *Deutsche Naturforscher und Ärzte*.

"The hat is moving even now in the fourth dimension," said Roussel.

"I don't see it."

"Nevertheless, it moves."

"Mumbo-jumbo!" Teddy Roosevelt boomed in his bulliest voice. "Tosh and bosh and biscuits!"

We were drinking gin and bitters in the Mombasa Hotel Bar. I had just finished telling him about my research into the nature of reality. He was in Africa with his son Kermit, killing things.

He advised me to "give it up. Leave profundity to the Princeton gang." He laid his big, double-barreled Holland on the table. "This will blow your flimsy philosophy to smithereens."

"What's behind it all?" I asked, letting anguish tinge my voice so as to move him, perhaps, to sympathy. "Do you know?"

"Bones—nothing but bones."

He downed his drink, then whispered, "And ghosts."

I asked him if he thought the dead might not come back to take their revenge on the living as they had on Winchester's widow.

"If they do," he said, "I can expect to be torn apart by wild beasts."

Tired, I returned to the harbor. Out on the water, the steamer swayed and in it Roussel at his writing desk, bravely refusing all news of the outside world. I looked once more at the red-roofed houses climbing the hill. The sun was setting, and their windows seemed to catch fire in the dying light. The wind was rising. It carried the odor of sandalwood and roses and with it women's laughter, like bells.

Tomorrow I will visit those women, provided their houses let me. But for now—a visit to Roussel's chiropractor! I said as I searched my pockets for his card. Perhaps he will be able to remedy the slight ache of existence—temporarily, until I climb the hill at first light.

If the sun should happen to rise once more.

THE SCOURGE OF DARKNESS

We sent for Edison, because of the darkness. The darkness had finally unnerved us. It was insupportable—the darkness at the heart. And so we sent for him, never believing for a moment that he would come, that *Edison* would come. Hoping, yes!—but full of doubt and mindful of our great presumption. But Africa made us extremely nervous. So we sent for him. "Come at once!" we telegraphed. "Come at once" in dots and dashes. And by God he came! We couldn't believe it. We could not believe that he would come. But he did—and faster, too, than any of us thought possible. He arrived within minutes of our telegraphing—his blue workman's jacket smoking, his hair standing on end, and the air crackling all around him.

"You sent for me," he said irritably.

We saw that he was tired: he had been working for three days without sleep in his West Orange laboratory to pry open the secret of the electric eel.

"Yes," we said sheepishly. "It's the darkness, you see—the accursed, infernal darkness. It makes us nervous."

We took off our safari hats and wrung them apologetically.

Edison walked up and down, studying the darkness. He did so with the air of a connoisseur, of a man who has looked at the dark and learned to appreciate its subtleties. He felt around in it like someone caressing velvet draperies.

We waited to hear what he would say—what *Edison* would say.

For a long while, he said nothing, only sighed—sighed a dark and velvety sigh that brought us to the edge of a swoon.

At last he asked for a towel with which to wipe the darkness from his hands.

"It is, indeed, dark," he said frowning.

We were glad to hear that we had not been mistaken.

"Yes, yes—this is no ordinary dark," he said.

We cheered him then and there for confirming what we had suspected but were never able to verify because of the taint on our judgment that came from years of exposure to Africa.

"I should like to measure it," he said decisively.

"By all means—measure it!" we assented.

We went to the rest house and watched through the window as Edison took the measure of our darkness with a special instrument. He made notes in a little book after each sighting. We admired his composure—how he did not flinch from the blackness that roiled about him. As he penetrated its most profound depths, he was enfolded; and we lost sight of him.

"Dear Mr. Edison!" we cried. And then we prayed, each of us in his own way, that the great man should not be obliterated.

Time passed; little by little our spirits fell.

He reappeared. He folded his instrument and beckoned to us.

We filed out, hardly daring to look him in the face.

"It is a darkness on a scale such as I have never before observed," he said, his voice trembling slightly. "I reckon it at -9.7; -10 is absolute darkness, which cannot be measured because the minimum illumination needed to read the instrument is .3." He paused, cleared his throat, and said, "Gentlemen, we are standing in the vestibule of absolute darkness."

We shuddered. We knew it was dark, but not *how* dark!

Exhausted, Edison returned with us to the rest house. We noticed that he was nervous and began to misgive. (Africa has such power to shake one!) He asked for broth, and we gave it to him. He asked that all the lanterns be lit, and we lit them.

"I wish I had my electric underwear," he said, "to pep me up."

"We have no electricity!" we exclaimed.

"But you telegraphed."

"With our minds. It's a little trick Quigley learned at the Institute for Psychical Research."

Edison fell silent, considering this new difficulty.

"Then you won't be able to illuminate our miserable darkness?"

"I didn't say that," he said.

He rose to his feet and went outside. He stood there a moment, confronting the vast indifference, then turned to us and shouted, "By God I will do it! I, Thomas Alva Edison, Scourge of Darkness, will do it!"

"Hooray!" we shouted, tossing our hats into the general obscurity.

Edison scooped up a bit of concentrated darkness that had collected around the base of a baobab tree and locked himself in the rest house (requisitioned as a laboratory) to experiment on it. During the ensuing hours, we heard screams; but whether they were Edison's or the dark's, we could not say.

That night (I refer to a temporal concept, not a perceptible event—day and night being indistinguishable where all is always dark) a haggard Edison emerged from the rest house. He spread his hands before him in a gesture of defeat.

"It cannot be done," he said.

We responded with groans.

For several days, Edison lay at the foot of the baobab tree. He did not speak. He did not move. We could not see his eyes—whether open or closed—in that thick murk. We feared he had caught the sleeping sickness and would remain dormant for months.

In despair, Toby committed a most dreadful suicide, much in use at the time: he opened his mouth wide and swallowed the darkness.

"I am drowning!" he cried at the last.

Captain Slade proposed a little comic relief "to lighten the situation," but we found his jest in poor taste.

We tightened the handkerchiefs around our mouths and withdrew.

Edison awoke with a bright idea. Thankfully for us he did not have the sleeping sickness: he had merely slept in the usual way of our kind.

"I think even in my sleep," he explained. "And I have thought profoundly of the dark."

We took heart.

"I'll capture it on *film*!" he announced, "then bury it under-ground in absolute darkness where it will be unable to escape—that darkness being greater than this by .3."

"Ha! Ha! Ha!" we laughed scornfully. "What an absurd idea!"

"Doubting Thomases!" he chided.

Ashamed of our bad manners, we went into the jungle and hid. When we returned to apologize, we found him chagrined.

"My movie camera is in New Jersey," he said.

Hanby recalled that Georges Méliès had left his camera behind after filming *An African Fantasy*. The porters parted with it reluc-tantly (and only after the promise of additional green umbrellas), believing it an instrument of magic.

We presented the camera to Edison and then, having come to the end of our strength, retired to the dining-tent for cocktails.

"My God, it's getting lighter!" we shouted. "Can it be he's done it after all?"

We left the dining-tent in search of Edison. We found him in a clearing. Darkness swirled about like smoke. Here and there it was thin enough to distinguish individual blades of grass.

"Look!" shouted Quigley. "Stars!"

The Stygian darkness had dispelled to such an extent that we could, indeed, see stars, which had long been hidden in obscurity.

"Betelgeuse, Rigel, and Sirius!" we cried.

As we stood and watched, the night turned gray and the stars were quenched by the feeble light.

"Edison!" we intoned, ready to exalt him. "Oh, Edison!"

But he was troubled.

"The operation was not a 100% success," he confessed sadly. "The dark is too palpable, too thick. You can see how it still clings to the walls of the rest house, the edges of the leaves, and to the backs of your hands."

He was right. It needed the sun, but the sun would not rise.

"But the worst is over," we said, trying to cheer him. "It's not nearly so dark as before."

"Gray!" moaned Edison, who loved clarity above all. "Everything is gray!"

"We can learn to live with 'gray,'" we said. "We can learn to love it!"

He shook his head and left us as inexplicably as he had arrived, leaving behind the acrid smell of electricity.

"Gray will soon be our favorite color!" we called after him, such was our joy, such was our gratitude.

But he had returned once more to daylight and the incandescent night.

Did we miss night? Some did. Quigley, Hanby, and others did, remembering, with a sentimental fondness, how they would retreat behind the shuttered windows of the rest house. Their long shadows had waved against the walls, while foxtrots crackled on the gramophone and white-coated house boys passed dreamily among them. Those who now missed the night had made for themselves a dream life and would gladly have returned to the darkness to dream again. They were depressed by unvarying gray days—neither day nor night but time only, which seemed unbearably present, oppressive, and slow. For my part, I found the grayness congenial, for in it I detected the bones of the world, all but invisible in blackness or in the blinding light. Was I a philosopher then? No; at that time, I was one who was fascinated by death.

Edison never returned to Africa, in spite of Quigley's distress calls. But once a crate arrived from Menlo Park, containing a machine to regulate light that would return to us—Edison declared in a brief note—the natural alternation of day and night. But the apparatus, mostly glass, was smashed beyond repair.

So we went on, there, in that way, that gray way, until the sun one morning did rise; and we resumed our lives as they had been before the darkness had engulfed us. And for a while, lived as you do.

But only for a while.

GROWING UNCERTAINTY

He wanted to teach arithmetic, he said. 1 + 1 = 2. Nothing more complicated. Certainly not the calculus, or elementary functions. Not even trigonometry. Arithmetic: 1 + 1 = 2. He would teach geometry, if we insisted; but only the two-dimensional sort. He could no longer cope with the third dimension, never mind the fourth. The thought that there might be a fifth made him want to lie down. He could also instruct us in the Cartesian equation, if we wished. He had graph paper. He had brought it from Zürich. Plotting coordinates he found restful. That is what he sought in Africa: restfulness. All this talk about uncertainty was destroying his nerves. God does not play dice, he said more than once. His marriage wasn't working either—he could see that. Mileva had her own ideas about the universe. She was becoming uncooperative. The scientific community was becoming uncooperative—even his hair wouldn't cooperate! To hell with it! he said, throwing away his comb. I'll use my fingers! Fingers are simpler. He had always loved simplicity, he said. What could be simpler than arithmetic?

"We're not interested," said Oates, who was drinking.

I looked sharply at him to remind him of what is due a guest.

"We're here to shoot elephants," he said brusquely. "And rhinoceros. And"—fixing me with a counter-look—"ignoramuses. We want tusks, you understand…ivory! We didn't come to Africa to do sums."

"You're drunk!" I said in a scalding tone.

"I'm a scientist," he smirked as he picked up his bottle and started for his tent. "And now if you'll excuse me, I'm off to study the effects of Bombay Gin on a 200-pound man."

His tent swallowed him up.

"I'm sorry, Albert."

"What about you?" he asked, offering me a rust-colored copybook.

"I'm interested in Zero," I told him. "In nothing."

"Never mind," he said, patting the back of my hand in the friendliest of ways. "I'll go into the wilderness and measure things. I have my ruler." He showed me it. "Measuring things is also restful, so long as they don't squirm and the ruler doesn't shrink or stretch. Can you guide me?"

"Yes."

I gave him a pith helmet and a porter. To carry his copybooks and his graph paper. His change of socks and violin.

"Is it far?" he asked.

"Yes."

"Good. I'm in the mood for a long walk."

I bent down and tied his shoelaces.

"Can we travel in a straight line?" he asked, and in his voice I detected a faint querulousness.

"If you like."

He liked. He was done with lines that bent—"the great curves of space." (He traced an elegant contour that reminded me of Anna.) All done. Straight lines were simpler, more restful.

"1 + 1 = 2," he said.

I wanted to tell him then and there that Africa was not the place for restfulness. I wanted to tell him how Africa made us all nervous, but I said nothing. He would find out for himself soon enough that Africa was neither restful nor simple.

Here, I thought, 1 + 1 does not always equal 2.

Here was not the place to recover from a nervous breakdown.

"Do you incline towards the Mechanical World View or the Electromagnetic?" Albert asked.

"I have no opinion," I answered.

"Very wise," he said.

We stopped for the night in a Nyika village. Albert asked the villagers if they would like arithmetic lessons. He would be happy, he said, to give them free of charge to any and all comers. The villagers said they were not interested in arithmetic. Their interest lay rather in the fields of sweet potatoes and peas.

Albert picked up his violin and began to play a folk melody he had learned in Milan.

(I thought of Arthur Conan Doyle playing in his tent by the river Potha while he dreamt of Moriarty.)

The villagers sat in a ring and wept at the sadness of the music. They called it "sorrowing."

Albert lifted his bow from the strings and entreated them: "Will you let me teach you arithmetic?"

"No," they said, "teach us to play the sorrowing."

Albert threw a leaf into the Tana. There were ants on the leaf. It drifted into the current, then sped downstream.

"Do you think those ants know they are moving?" he asked.

"Decidedly," I said.

"Why not us? Why not the human ants on the enormous leaf that is forever sailing through space?"

I gave him my most indifferent shrug to let him know that I did not care for this. It was, however, lost on him.

"Could it be our frame of reference travels with us as it does not in the case of those ants?"

He was making me tired—tired and irritable.

"I thought you wanted to rest!" I snapped.

He hung his head sheepishly and mumbled through his mustache about old habits.

Albert crawled about the wilderness, measuring things. He kept a careful record of his measurement. He would slap the ruler down along the edge of the thing he wanted to measure, squint at it, lick the end of his pencil, then write a figure in his notebook. Its pages were black with his pencilings.

"How's it coming, Albert?"

He frowned.

"Ask me tomorrow after I have re-measured what I measure today. If nothing has changed, I will be upheld."

"You must wear your topi, Albert. The sun will addle your brains."

"That would be good," he said, and laughed.

One night he played the violin so sweetly the world held its breath.

At least that is how it seemed to me.

"It is nice to sit still," he said.

"Why do you think so much, Albert?"

"Restlessness."

He slept for three days and nights, but woke unrefreshed.

"Thinking has become a curse for me," he said. "I think even when asleep."

Like Edison, I thought.

I took Albert to meet the wild forest people. Pennington, whom they idolized, hung from a pole in a clearing.

"These are the wild forest people," I told Albert. "And this is my friend Pennington, who had his throat cut by a porter. They have made a fetish of him—he brings them luck."

"I envy him his rest," Albert said sadly.

"They would do as much for you," I remarked.

"Modesty prevents me from accepting."

"Are you happy, Albert?"

"Happy is a relative term," he said.

Africa is constantly unraveling. Like one of Albert's woolen sweaters, it is forever coming apart. Whether from insects or rot or humidity or one of the little-understood mechanical processes of deterioration—Africa collapses, molders, falls to pieces only to be replaced by a new Africa indistinguishable from the old which, in its turn, collapses, molders, falls to pieces.

Ad infinitum.

It is this that made me nervous. The terrifying energy! Matter ceaselessly transforming itself. A world that does not rest, that denies the very possibility of rest. At times I almost longed for the sleeping sickness.

"Why don't you leave?" Albert asked.

"Africa has rooted in me—it has grown right through me. You would have to tear it out of my heart."

He nodded. He was a scientist, but he understood the power of metaphor.

"This morning when I took my measurements I noticed that things had changed during the night."

Now it was my turn to nod for I understood that, overnight, things squirm, the meterstick molts.

"Africa," I said simply, to a man who valued simplicity above all.

"Africa is making me nervous," he admitted; and as if to confirm his self-appraisal, one of his eyelids twitched.

Then, as if in spiteful mimicry, Africa twitched: the sharp grass pierced the veldt, the Tana jumped its banks, elephants trampled the villages and shambas of sweet potatoes and peas, it snowed on Mt. Kenya while everywhere the darkness deepened and the wind sorrowed.

"Light a fire!" cried Albert, pulling on a second sweater to stop his teeth from chattering.

Attracted by the fire, an immeasurable column of safari ants plundered our encampment, carrying off Albert's notebook, his pencil, and ruler. They would have made off with his violin if I had not snatched it from their path.

"Arithmetic is of no use here," Albert lamented.

"It's a dicey business," I agreed.

"Does the energy of a man persist after death in a form that can be said to be uniquely his?" Albert asked earnestly.

We were burying Oates, who had been devoured by the marauding ants.

"If you mean: does Oates still exist elsewhere?... I don't know."

"Neither do I," said Albert, whose once firm belief in science's ability to discover the mysterious workings of the universe had by now all but extinguished.

"Dig!" I urged him. I was keen to get Oates underground, because of the heat.

"I like the word *elsewhere*," said Albert, with surprising sentimentality.

The scrape of our shovels against the flinty soil refuted for me the idea of "elsewhere."

"Do you think the ants were avenging their comrades drowned in the Tana?" he asked after a silence.

"Will you never stop asking questions?" I shouted.

"I have no answers anymore," he said as he took up his violin and played.

"Neither does Oates," I remarked dryly.

"I am thinking of Ulm," said Albert. "I was a child in Ulm."

I was in no mood for childhood reminiscence.

"The light in which I played as a child in Ulm is traveling toward the edge of the universe where it will curve and one day return, carrying the image of myself as a child that was constituted by that light. So that one day I will again be a child playing in Ulm."

I turned away, believing him mad.

"What do you think: could the light be 'elsewhere'? Could light be our afterlife?"

"You're insane!" I shouted and regretted it immediately, seeing his wounded look.

"Isaac Newton was insane for a while. Why not me?"

"Remember the leaf I threw in the Tana?" Albert asked. "What made it fall?"

"Gravity," I said.

"What *caused* it to fall?"

"Death," I said.

"Did it expend its energy in falling, or was it drained of it before it fell? Is that what caused it to fall? It simply let go, no longer having the strength to cling to the tree. Where did its energy go? Into the tree? The air? Into the ground? Is that what gravity is—the accumulated lost energies of the dead things of this world?"

"You should go home," I muttered.

"I came here to rest from civilization and its complicated social interactions."

"Africa is no place to rest," I said wearily.

"*Objects at rest tend to remain at rest until acted upon by some external force*—Newton's First Law."

"Africa is a force…" I said with an intimation of menace.

"You should have let me teach you arithmetic!" he shouted.

"And here is a force to send you home!"

I knocked him rudely down.

He rose to his feet and clapped the dust from his hands.

"Africa does not exist," he declared. "If it did, it would affirm universal constants. No such affirmation is evident. I propose to search for the unifying principle in all things and leave Africa to

Heisenberg and the disciples of Uncertainty." He felt his shoulder gingerly. "You ought not to have knocked me down."

"Edison failed here, too," I said, wanting suddenly to comfort him.

"Light bulbs and phonographs! Ticker tape machines and moving picture shows!" sneered Albert. "What are they next to *that*!" He gestured broadly with his hand, taking in the universe (all but Africa, which—it was understood—is an illusion). "Toys!"

Albert went. He stepped into one of Africa's many black holes and was gone. (While they have not yet been discovered, they exist all the same.) He came out the other side, as he ought, in light. Darkness is foreign to him; he did not belong here. Perhaps now he is in Ulm, hunting frogs along the banks of the Danube. Or a baby at his mother's breast. Or perhaps he is an old man getting ready to climb into his death bed.

I did not know, nor did I wish to.

I wasn't sorry to see Albert go. His helpless questioning increased my nervousness. Years before, I had resolved to ask no more, knowing full well it is senseless to question Africa. In the presence of so much that cannot be explained, one is relieved of the necessity (misery) of inquiry.

One rests or is nudged from rest.

One sleeps or goes on safari.

One acts or is acted upon, as the case may be.

In accordance with the divine law of indifference.

RAISING PENNINGTON

I learned to raise the dead from an old juju man. Why he made me a present of the mystery of mysteries I don't know. Perhaps he hoped to empty the next world of white men, having had—he said in Kikuyu—a bellyful of them in this. I was grateful. You recall Pennington, whom I esteemed as a friend despite his appetite for native women, had his throat cut "ear to ear" by a mutinous porter. The long safari days lacked savor in his absence, and so I resolved to put the secret of resurrection to the test on my dead chum.

I went to the wild forest people, who had made an idol of him. He was in excellent condition, dry and intact. Thankfully, his head

remained atop his neck, else all the charms in the world would not
have raised him. Despite his venerable status, I purchased him with
a minimum of haggling for a dozen green umbrellas and a full-length
portrait of Taft. The portrait was especially admired and hotly con-
tested by two natives, each claiming to have unearthed Pennington
after his hasty interment. (We had feared new outrages at the hands
of the porters and were eager to be on our way.)

"Sir, the fat man rightfully belongs to me as it was I who found
Mr. Pennington while digging for turnips," said one in perfect mission English.

"This black man is crazy!" shouted his rival for the President's
lovingly rendered obesity. "I discovered him while digging for yams!"

They would have come to blows had not a meteor fallen on
them, putting an end to their disagreeable wrangling.

The chief of the wild forest people divided the portrait between
the widows—an excellent settlement, I thought. I put Pennington
under my arm (he weighed little, was stiff and easy to carry) and ran
to the rest house where I intended to recite the savage syllables. (I'm
sorry, but I cannot divulge them. Not even Houdini will pry the
secret from my lips!)

Before I could finish, the Bishop appeared and reviled me.

"Sacrilege! Abomination and horror!" he whinnied. "The road
to the afterlife isn't a boulevard to stroll to and fro. The dead had
best stay dead."

In no mood to argue, I wrapped him up in his skirts and thrashed
him with a carpet beater.

"Unnatural monster!" he shrieked. "Perversion of nature!"

I thumped him once more for good measure, then pushed him
out the door into a nearby slough.

I threw Pennington over my shoulders and ran all the way to
Mombasa. I now had the wild idea of exhibiting my new-found

powers in the Mombasa Club to vex Mr. Willoughby—chief detractor of my past researches into the heart of Africa, belittling them as "lacking scientific rigor." Here is rigor of the first order, I said to myself—meaning Pennington, who in his extremity embodied the ultimate in rigor.

I entered without challenge despite my odd-looking parcel. (The Mombasa Club has been witness to far worse. You have only to recall the spontaneous combustion of the Polish courier during port and cigars, the lion in the cloakroom, or the half-naked Masai trailing a bundle of black strings across the foyer, his hair dressed in red mud.)

Mr. Willoughby crackled his newspaper resentfully.

"How dare you disturb our meditations!" he barked.

Brigadier Craig, who had served with distinction in India, vilified me for having failed to wipe my feet before treading the African dust over "our portion—our bit of civilization."

Undaunted, I put Pennington on the snooker table.

"Take that dirty thing away!" the majordomo fulminated as he beat a gong into the already tense atmosphere.

The members threw up their hands in disgust.

"Prepare to witness the extraordinary!" I shouted.

Something in my tone must have convinced them of the seriousness of my purpose for they laid down their arms.

"The man you see before you is dead," I continued theatrically.

I invited them to assure themselves of the truth of the matter. They did in spite of Pennington's patently unwholesome condition. They held a mirror to his blackened lips and tickled his feet with an ostrich feather. Try as they might they could not get a rise out of him; not so much as a twitch.

"This man was murdered, buried, dug up, and made a fetish by the wild forest people. In life he was my friend, and I have been given the words to restore him once again to the living."

Their skepticism gave way to astonishment as I began Pennington's resuscitation. I spoke the words softly into his ear, to safeguard them from the gentlemen of the Mombasa Club, who were sure to abuse them given the opportunity.

Pennington opened his eyes.

The gentlemen gasped.

"What have you done?" he asked as he looked about him at the horns bristling on the club-room walls. He worked his jaw a moment to get the stiffness out and repeated the question, this time with feeling: "For God's sake, what have you done!"

"I've brought you back to life, man!" I cried in exasperation.

"Meddler! Philanthropist! I was perfectly content as an idol. I was treated with the utmost respect."

Pritchett, chief of the Mombasa constabulary, had been summoned to put down the insurrection. He arrived with a troop of askari policemen.

"There is no insurrection," I said scornfully.

Pritchett referred to his notebook:

"'Insurrection at the Mombasa Club,' reported shortly after 2 o'clock." He looked at his watch. "It is now a quarter past." He looked to me as if expecting applause for his efficiency. I offered none.

"Resurrection!" I screamed instead. "There has been a resurrection."

"Resurrection, *in*surrection—it amounts to the same thing," the imperturbable Pritchett replied. "Both are in violent opposition to the established order; as such, they are illegal."

He escorted me to the courthouse where I was given a stiff fine. Pennington, who bore still the marks of his rough burial, created a sensation in the street.

"There is also the matter of the Bishop," said the judge after I had paid for Pennington.

"What about the Bishop?" I asked innocently.

"His majesty has been sullied."

The Bishop took the stage with his muddied surplice as "evidence." I was about to denounce him as a prig but was brutally gaveled down by his Lordship.

I paid—exorbitantly—for my happy desecration of the Bishop and left without another word.

I returned Pennington to the wild forest people. They gave me back the green umbrellas but refused to part with either half of Taft. I suspect the image of his immense corporeality nourished their dreams, which are said to be vivid. They were ecstatic and quickly gave Pennington back the death I had deprived him of, if only temporarily. He seemed happy as he suffered their exaltation. For my part, I felt decidedly let down.

"It ought to have been a *coup de théâtre*," I complained to Sarah Bernhardt, whom Wilde, then the world, called "Divine."

She had just reprised her legendary performance in a revival of *La dame aux camélias* behind the same proscenium arch where Pavlova had danced for us (and won the affection of Captain Slade). The Kikuyus did not respond to the play: they are a stolid people, slow to make a public demonstration of the movements of the heart.

"One never knows how our work will be received," Mme. Bernhardt sighed. "If we did, there would be no flops in the theater."

She coughed into Camille's blood-stained handkerchief.

"Your dead friend does have a certain *je ne sais quoi*," she continued. "Rather more now that he's dead, I think, though I did not know him before."

I could not argue. Though I loved Pennington, his debauched life had been a secret shame to me, who am certainly no prude as my relations with Anna and Mrs. Willoughby attest.

The wild forest people carried Pennington into the wilderness. I would not see him alive again, though, from time to time, I would see him dead: under a juniper tree, in an alley, or a swamp with the moonlight on his face. I think he meant me well. I think he appeared to me during times of great unease to make me easy in my mind. To convey to me mutely that this life, from which he departed twice, is the shadow of the next. To safari me, if I should desire it, into his country. Though I have been tempted, there was something in his face—a sadness which holds me back. Even so, I would have gone with him after leaving the City of Radiant Objects if Wilbur had not taken me to America in his aeroplane (in what Freud would later call "my flight from death").

"The wild forest people have a much healthier attitude towards these things," Mme. Bernhardt said in ringing tones. Though an old woman, she retained her bell-like voice. "They aren't so afraid of death."

She shivered uncontrollably; I would have lit a fire for her, but the night was warm.

"It will come to me soon," she said, her voice betraying her emotion.

She looked to me as if for a cue—a word that she might answer and so keep the dialogue going; but I did not know this play, if play it was. She fell silent, letting the camellias drop from her hands.

"I would see you home," I said, embarrassed, "but I must stay here. In Africa. My work…"

She waved away my explanations.

"Paris is not so pleasant this time of year," she said, walking towards the Indian Ocean.

The next day she was to begin filming *La dame aux camélias,* which I would later see in Cincinnati with the King of all the Belgians. (Or was that a dream?)

"Nothing is real," she called from the rail of her private steamship. "All is theater—even your friend, his death, his deification—theater."

She dropped the blood-stained handkerchief into the harbor. The blood was not real. The harbor seemed to be real, but I may have been mistaken. These things are difficult. Sometimes I feel the world slipping away. These things are difficult to tell. Albert knows; he tried to measure it. Tried and failed.

"*Adieu!*" Mme. Bernhardt cried over the throbbing of the engines.

In a little while (less than I would have thought possible!), the ship crossed the horizon, leaving nothing but a black plume of smoke to mark its place. Soon that, too, disappeared.

"Life is an illusion," she said from beyond the horizon.

(How is it possible I heard?)

"The illusion, however, is terribly attractive."

Her voice ceased.

I turned from the ocean as the light went out of the sky and walked into Africa—into its jungle where the illusion is most powerful of all.

A lion roared. A tree exploded into a shower of golden birds.

I crouched in terror of a lion that might or might not be real and waited.

THE CITY OF RADIANT OBJECTS

The first thing one sees on entering the City of Radiant Objects is a field of white beds. It is here that all the trajectories of the walkers converge: mysteriously as it came, the walking sickness leaves them, and they lie down and sleep for days. It is here also that the sleepers awake at last from the sleeping sickness. My God, they say, have I been asleep so long? They cast off the dreaming in which they have been mired, many for years—cast it off without interpretation, so great is their joy in the sudden clarity of the air.

In the City of Radiant Objects, things are free of the obligation to signify. It is this that makes them radiant. And it is for this I have been searching so long in Africa without knowing it.

"It began with a vision of an iron stairway," he said, fingering the silver plumb he wore around his neck. "It made a graceful S in the air above Alexandria where I was engaged in scholarly research at the great Library." To illustrate, he traced with a finger a graceful S in the air above the tiled esplanade.

I was giving praise to the Architect of the Radiant City beneath a perfectly formed plane tree. The reason I was giving him praise ought to be obvious. Isn't it? Well, consider who he was and may very well be yet. Standing in the Alexandrine gardens of the third century AD, he had imagined this place—imagined it, then caused it to be built here in equatorial Africa, with a single stroke of genius. What else if not genius for he used no tools. He created ideal forms out of nothing with not so much as a speck of dust left over to mark their making. Was he not worthy of my praise?

"I started with a spiral stair and ended with a sill on which many since have placed their elbows in rapt contemplation of perfection."

"Why here?" I asked. "Why not in some more temperate zone?"

"I wanted a place devoid of associations," he answered. "And one in which objects would cast no shadow."

He lifted his arm and the wide mandarin sleeve fell back, revealing a hand that cast no shadow under the vertical tropic rays.

"It's a property of the equatorial sun," he said. "Only shadowless objects can be radiant."

He looked down at my shoes, scuffed and dusty with the journey.

"You must keep them well polished," he said of them.

I walked through the City, inventorying its architectural features: Window.

Fluted column.

Architrave.

Proscenium arch.

Plinth.

Oriel.

Stone balustrade.

Golden dome.

"No," said the Architect, ripping the list to pieces. "This is not the way to experience objects."

He called for the movers.

"You must immerse yourself—not entertain them one at a time."

The movers arrived with numerous objects and piled them on top of me. Because the objects were light, they did not hurt me.

"It is the meanings people give things that make them heavy," the Architect said from outside the mound in which I lay buried. "Objects in themselves weigh nothing at all."

I rummaged in them a while.

"Do you see the radiance of the whole?" he asked.

"I see it," I replied.

I pillowed my head on a soft catafalque and rested.

"You know the phrase 'shades of meaning'?" he asked, pursuing his catechism.

"Yes," I said, stifling (I confess) a yawn.

"It is literally true. Shadows are meanings made visible. Radiant objects cast none. They are light."

I permitted several small objects to enter me for my spiritual well-being. While there was no pain, neither was there enlightenment.

"Chairs will float if one has never thought of sitting on them."

Indeed, I had seen a dozen or so chairs high above the Museum of Exquisite Machines as I approached the City.

"A sea is vast, cold, and desolate; but it is only thinking that makes it so."

"Yes," I said. "There is a sea here with me now, and it is very pleasant, and so are the fish swimming in it."

"Do you fear drowning?" he asked, testing me.

"Not at all," I answered confidently, for I really didn't.

"Good," he said. "The sea in itself is not in the least frightening. It is only the idea of drowning that makes it so."

"Mozart is also here," I said.

"Of course," he answered. "His music has always been here."

We were sitting once more beneath the plane tree (not on a chair!). While it cast no shadow (how could it?), I had the sensation of shade. The movers had removed the objects. And while I had felt no discomfort beneath them, I was glad to be "out in the air" again, for it was the crystalline air of the City of Radiant Objects more than the objects themselves that amazed me.

"The air is like a—"

The Architect cut me short.

"We do not allow similes here," he said, "nor any figurative language, which distracts from the object, thereby dimming its radiance."

He blindfolded me and had me identify objects by touch or smell "to strengthen you in objectness." He bid me taste certain objects, cleansing my palate each time with sherbet. Many were delicious, others foul-tasting, depending on the material. The end of all these trials was an increased sensitivity to the true nature of things that remains with me even now.

"Why are there so few people here?" I asked, looking around me, as if for the first time.

"People cannot resist giving meaning to things," he said. "*I was sitting in that very chair when the wind arrived with the fragrance of frangipani from the South. Or, I was holding that tortoise comb when I thought of Rachel, whom I had once loved long ago. Or, I leaned against that column and recalled a picnic on the beach at Crete.* And for those people, for ever after, 'chair' and 'comb' and 'column' adumbrate qualities foreign to their nature as objects. Once that happens, radiance is at risk."

"And so you ask them to leave?"

"They leave without being told. We wake and find them gone. They understand."

"Cannot memory also make a thing radiant?" I asked.

I was thinking of Anna, whose face shone in my memory though she was now, like me, no longer young.

"Only falsely," he answered. "Memory is kind or cruel but seldom truthful."

"And desire?" I asked.

"Desire is a projection of one's need upon an object."

"And can there be love where there are no objects of desire?"

He turned and looked into the distance. What perfection he saw there I do not know.

We sat for a time in silence. I waited for the sun to set, but it did not.

FLIGHT

I fled the City of Radiant Objects and hurried into the waiting dark. The merciless logic of the Architect and his city, brilliant under a never-setting sun, had injured sensitive tissue so that I craved the bandages of shade and shadow. My head ached and my eyes stung. My mouth was bitter with the taste of disappointment. I had hoped to escape the weight and waste of matter, the endless variations on a theme of procreation. I had longed for the economy of the ark floating above a drowned world of useless diversity. But the purity of the City was intolerable, its idealism inhuman. I could not live without desire, love, and night—without the sweet disorder of Anna's hair.

"Hello," said Wilbur as I entered the clearing. "Would you like to ride in my new aeroplane?"

"Why yes," I said.

He was leaning against a juniper tree, eating a sandwich.

"Where is Orville?" I asked, for I understood they were inseparable.

"In Dayton," he answered, "looking after the shop. I came to Paris to drum up money for our machine. The night was so beautiful I thought I'd fly to Africa."

"They will wonder where you've gone," I said.

"Paris is asleep. All of France is asleep. Only Wilbur is awake."

He slept little, he said, because of his mind; it revolved constantly with diagrams and formulae. His mind, he said, gave him great pleasure. His mind, he said, wrought the most elegant science.

He sang a jaunty song, accompanying himself on the piano-wire braces of his aeroplane. In return, the jungle performed a delicate score for winds and nightingale.

Silence once more restored, we stood under the moon, smiling at one another. I was tempted to go off into the trees with him, but only for a moment.

I coughed instead, to break the spell.

"I flew through the night," he said. "I felt the land under me and then the ocean. The ocean was blacker than the land and lit here and there with the tiny lights of ships. And then Africa—its welcoming darkness. I landed my machine here among the thorns without a single tear to its paper wings. How do you explain that?"

I couldn't. Instead, I quoted Victor Hugo: "'The enigma in which being dissolves.'"

I admired aloud the various features of his aeroplane.

"The engine's a dream," he said. "I have only to close my eyes."

I began to cry for reasons I have never understood. Perhaps the softness of the night, the strangeness of the machine, the beauty of science and the moon.

The wild forest people came out from behind the trees and began to dance. My friend Pennington, whose throat had been cut by the porters, was with them. His face was white, but that may have been the effect of moonlight. Wilbur looked on benevolently. His oiled sandwich paper shone in the grass. How lovely everything was at that moment! The imaginary Haha bird sat on a pine bough just as it did on the Chinese scroll hanging in Quigley's tent. Where is Quigley? I wondered. And Carlson, Hanby, Stephens, and Captain Slade? What has happened to the journey upon which we embarked with full hearts so long ago?

I took off my clothes and joined the wild forest people in their dance.

"Is this what you want?" asked Wilbur, getting into his machine.

"I don't know!" I cried in an anguished voice.

He started his motor.

"That man is dead, you know," he called above the noise. "In a little while he will start to stink."

I tried to leave the dance, but the dancers had formed a charmed circle around me.

"Goodbye," said Wilbur.

"Take me with you!" I shouted. "To Paris. To America and to Anna in the Hamptons!"

But the aeroplane was gone—I won't say "vanished," although that is the impression with which I was left. I heard the roar of the motor, the humming of the wires, then silence. The wild forest people went back into the trees, carrying Pennington with them.

I dressed quickly and left for Mombasa.

A herd of zebras rushed through the streets of Mombasa. I stepped into an alley, so as not to be trampled. They did only minor damage to the streetlights and the steeple of the Episcopal church. The people of Mombasa leaned out of their windows and cheered them.

"Hooray!" they shouted.

"*Qua-ha-ha*!" barked the zebras.

A woman waved to me from a house across the street.

"Come and drink with me," she called.

I waited for the zebras to pass, then crossed the street to her house. She was French; I am an American. We drank bumpers of champagne in honor of democracy.

"I am Madame Tussaud," she said. "My husband went into the jungle to discover a new orchid and never returned. I am hungry for kisses."

I kissed her. Why should she go hungry?

We opened the curtains and encouraged the moonlight to fall on the bed. Particles of it got all over us as we rolled on top of the sheet. Outside in the Mombasa night, the zebras whinnied joyously.

Night, I said, is what I like best.

She told me her house: Sagittarius; in China, the Monkey.

I fell asleep and dreamt I was flying in Wilbur's machine.

"Is that what you want?" asked Wilbur.

He was standing at the open window. His teeth flashed, his eyes sparkled. Stardust and broken bits of moon clung to his hair.

"What a handsome man!" exclaimed Madame Tussaud from the depths of sleep. Her face was white, but that may have been the effect of moonlight.

"Is that what you want?" he repeated.

"I don't seem to be able to leave!" I cried again in anguish. "How did you find me?"

"The zebras. Get dressed; we're flying to Dayton tonight. You'll work in the bicycle shop, tightening spokes. Anna can join you there."

I dressed and followed him out into the street. The wings of his machine trembled lightly in the wind. The wind strummed the wires.

Kassitura! I said to myself. How can I leave your magic harping?

Wilbur laid his hand on my arm. He spoke kindly: "We'll be there in no time. I've reshaped the propellers to a new equation. You have only to close your eyes."

We rolled down the street and jumped into the sky. The motor dreamed; the varnished propellers scarcely disturbed the sleeping town. The zebras drowsed under the mimosas. Madame Tussaud floated in the dark waters of sleep, and I was in flight from Africa.

Is this what I want? I asked myself.

I could not answer. For the second time that night I wept.

LONGING FOR AFRICA

We flew into Dayton through a thin pane of music. It's the music of America, said Wilbur. It's the music of get-up-and-go, he said. He was happy to be home. But I was having second thoughts. Already I missed the breathing of the jungle and the tom-tom pulse of Africa.

We landed in a fairground, trailing rags of red and green seaweed acquired at sea, along with a coat of salt that sparkled on our wings in the vivid Ohio sun. Wilbur had fallen asleep at the controls, and we would surely have perished had not our dipping wings splashed water in his face. I do not blame him: the flight from Africa to Ohio is long, as the map will prove to you beyond a doubt. How

I managed to hold on to the straps for so many nights is a mystery. Wilbur flew only at night so that he might practice his celestial navigation. Don't ask what we did during the daylight hours, because I can't remember.

We bounced along the midway and came to rest by a circus tent, topped with smartly snapping flags. An elephant trumpeted a greeting and, despite its silly hat, a longing for Africa jumped up strong in me. Though I had been stung and bitten, lost and clawed, I missed it still.

"Take me back," I said.

"It will be years before there is regular passenger service to Africa," said Wilbur. "We flew entirely by unscientific means, which cannot be duplicated."

The sun blared in the Ohio sky. The band played "My Fox Trot Girl" until the wind blew into the bandstand and scattered the music on the lawn. Women drifted like small white clouds across the grass as a crowd of men in derbies rushed to ogle our machine, wings yellow with pollen.

Oh, how I missed the pleasant gardens of Mombasa and the breeze that nightly rose from the Indian Ocean.

"Come," said Wilbur, taking my arm. "Orville is waiting."

The brothers walked through the streets of Dayton in long black coats and derbies. They walked silently, hands in pockets, their heads wreathed in sunlight. As I followed them about the city, I saw their potential as heroic monuments.

Bouquets arrived almost daily from the princes of Europe. The house where the brothers lived with their father and sister was mobbed with flowers whose confusion of perfumes made me dizzy. Boxes of cigars also arrived and these the brothers distributed on their walks, having early on renounced tobacco as well as strong spirits. That they were chaste goes without saying, and the women they received as gifts from various sultanates were found respectable situations in the homes of the brothers' many admirers.

"While you were in France, I gave a demonstration flight for the army that lasted 70 minutes," said Orville.

"I flew all the way from Africa," said Wilbur.

"Yes, but that doesn't count," said Orville, "because you used magic."

"True," said Wilbur.

I worked in the brothers' bicycle shop, tightening spokes and polishing the bicycle lanterns while the brothers were in Washington, selling their machine.

"It will make an excellent war machine," they said, "for the war that is coming."

"What war?" I asked, but they only winked and would say no more.

Anna had joined me from the Hamptons (by train) and we were happy for a time, living in the back of the shop. We found the smell of oiled chains piquant and would close the shop in the afternoon to make love.

"Do you still long for Africa?" she asked me as she rolled her stockings down her legs, a sight that never failed to arouse.

"No," I lied.

The brothers were famous all over the world, but fame did not turn their heads. They still walked the streets of Dayton, preoccupied by the arithmetic of flight. Sometimes, they would stop and loudly debate some aeronautical issue. The passersby smiled. They understood that their future was in some obscure way linked to the brothers; if not their future, their children's.

I was becoming increasingly unhappy. I wanted to return to Africa, but Anna kept a careful watch over me. She need not have bothered: I was broke, and it would take years working in the bicycle shop to save enough money for the boat fare.

"I wish Africa would sink into the ocean!" she shouted as I moped about.

For all I know it may have.

I began to suspect the whole thing was a dream. Anna was not, I soon realized, as I remembered her. For one thing, she wore no underwear; and while my years of absence on the Dark Continent might account for a change of fashion, what could account for the buckets of pistachio ice cream she consumed when I knew quite well she was allergic to pistachios! And the bicycles! At the end of three months every man, woman, and child in Dayton was astride one of the brothers' black bicycles and yet I don't recall having sold a single one! And the brothers themselves: increasingly, I had difficulty telling them apart. Wilbur was bald and his brother was not, but they seldom removed their hats. And why did it never rain in Dayton? And why did the band invariably play "My Fox Trot Girl" when I went to the fairground to examine the petrified elephant dung? All this, of course, is nothing to the flight from Africa itself. How can one explain such a technologically inexplicable event?

"Am I dreaming?" I asked Wilbur or Orville.

"Pinch yourself," one of them said.

But I was afraid.

"I'm thinking of leaving you," Anna said one afternoon, as we were lying on the bed in the back room of the bicycle shop.

I said nothing.

She sat up so that the sheet slipped from her charming breasts.

"Did you hear me?" she asked.

"Of course."

"You're incorrigible!" she said angrily, covering herself. "You will not stop thinking of Africa!"

"But I'm not!" I protested.

"You were seen at the fairgrounds, studying the elephant dung. A man of your age!"

She was disgusted, she said. She had had enough, she said. She would go back to the Hamptons and forget me, she said.

For the second time I said nothing.

"Well?" she demanded.

"Do you think this could be a dream?"

She scratched my face in reply.

I went to the sink and looked at my face in the mirror. There were scratches, but couldn't they have been made by some wild beast? Might I not be asleep in my tent under the Southern Cross?

"It proves nothing," I told her.

"Fool!" she sneered.

After the brothers had left for Europe, I found a note on my pillow:

> Anna is right: you are a fool. Remember Pennington, whose throat was cut. Remember Madam Tussaud, whose face was white. They are dead. They wanted you to keep them company through the long night. Is that what you want? Your Africa is a savage, backward place. It is better that you remain in Dayton. We will turn the bicycle shop over to you. If Anna leaves, we shall give you our sister's hand in marriage. Think about it: you could do worse.
>
> Cordially,
> Wilbur

Terrible longing for Africa!

I am building an aeroplane, using the brothers' latest plan. Now that Anna is gone, I have all afternoon to work. I confess to missing her, but I miss Africa more. When I am there, I will think of her in the Hamptons, and that will be enough. Besides, there are lovely women in Mombasa and Nairobi—there are lovely women everywhere. (The brothers' sister, alas, is not one of them.)

"Such a trip is technically impossible," said the reporter from the *Dayton Herald*, who came to interview me. "I telegraphed the brothers, and they agree."

He rattled a flimsy telegraph in my face.

"I have only to close my eyes," I said, smiling mysteriously.

"Crackpot!" he shouted, slamming the door behind him.

I pulled the shade and set to work on a navigation instrument of my own design, containing dried elephant dung. With it I will find my way to Africa—or rather my aeroplane will, for I'll be asleep. I'll wake over the green islands, unless Africa is a dream and I drown.

THE ANGUISH OF HOUDINI

Houdini had just finished his famous cabinet escape at the Hansa Theatre when news arrived that I had raised Pennington. The escapologist flew immediately from Hamburg to Africa in his new French Voisin boxed-wing biplane. (You object that this is hardly possible: that the Voisin might have been capable of reaching the River Elbe from the military parade ground outside Hamburg but certainly not Africa! Will you never understand that anything is possible where Africa is concerned?)

"Is it true you've done a Lazarus?" Houdini asked, pulling off his insect-spattered goggles.

"Pardon me?"

"Raised the dead!" he shouted, so great was his impatience.

"Only once, and the 'Lazarus,' as you call him, wasn't happy."

Houdini looked as if he might go mad. I would not have been at all surprised had he rolled in the dust, or gibbered like a gibbon.

"Then it's true!" he shouted.

He rubbed his hands together in a visible display of exultation.

"If a single instance is enough to make it so, then yes—it is," I replied, not at all impressed by this excitable dandy in his pointed brown-and-white shoes.

"You must show me how it's done!" he said, opening his wallet and spilling a variety of colorful currency onto the African plain.

I sat in my tent, listening to Victor Herbert and Rudolf Friml rolls. The player piano was a gift from Albert Einstein, whom I'd once had the pleasure of escorting through Africa.

Houdini stood outside the tent and wheedled, "I'll do anything you want if you'll only teach me the trick of resurrection!"

I shied an old boot towards the tent flap.

"You can have my Voisin…?" he cajoled, undeterred.

"I dislike aviation!"

(You have only to recall my desperate flight from Mombasa on the wing of Wilbur's flying-machine to know why.)

"How about a pretty young girl to play with? You must be lonely living the life of a—what is it you *do* do here?"

"Adventurous, outdoor things," I said. I was determined to keep silent about the audacious, *metaphysical* things I did in Africa.

"A lonely life."

"I don't like women," I lied, unwilling to fall under any obligation to this ridiculous "magician."

"And boys?" he leered.

I threw the other boot.

"Watch this!" Houdini called.

He climbed into the packing crate in which my player piano had arrived from Switzerland; and Ali, my once faithful tent boy, nailed the lid shut. I bitterly resented Houdini's appropriation of one of the porters. Ali pushed the crate off the cliff, and together we watched it splash into the Indian Ocean.

"That's that," I said, with no little satisfaction.

But when I returned to my tent, Houdini was already there.

"Will you show me the secret now?" he screamed.

"You are dripping on my Turkish carpet," I said, turning away to hide my fury.

"Why not?" Houdini asked, lifting the mosquito net.

He had waked me in the middle of the night to resume his siege.

"The dead are cranky—they have nothing to say to us. They are disappointing company and ungrateful. They guard their secrets closely."

Not to be dissuaded, he crawled into bed with me.

"I'll introduce you to the crowned heads of Europe," he promised.

"I'm from Cincinnati!" I bristled. "We are unmoved by crowned heads."

"I'll trade you all my secrets for just this one."

"No!"

He ran outside and jumped into a quagmire. I watched him disappear beneath the moonlit muck. But next morning, he was there, in the dining-tent, eating an alligator-egg omelet and stinking of swamp. He looked at me in mute appeal; I returned his gaze without flinching.

He brought me a dead rabbit.

"Just a small revival?" he begged.

I shook my head no.

He brought me a foot.

"Make it dance!" he beseeched.

I closed my eyes and pretended to sleep.

He brought me a finger.

"Just the tiniest twitch of life?" he implored.

He set himself on fire and jumped into the Indian Ocean with rocks in his pockets. Later, I passed him on the trail to the bathing-machine, his eyebrows singed and his face black with soot.

"I can escape everything but death itself," he said disconsolately.

"I'm sorry, I cannot help you."

He went into the bathing-machine and wept.

Why *not* give him the secret? I wasn't pledged to secrecy, nor had the Kikuyu man who taught me the art of resurrection imposed such a condition. True, my experience with Pennington had been disagreeable; but that in itself was not reason enough to conceal it from Houdini. Did I dislike Houdini? Neither more nor less than I disliked anyone else. Why then did I so stubbornly refuse to grant him what he so desperately sought? Was it the use he would make of it—resurrection as vaudeville routine? Was this my only scruple? I was not religious; I had, at times, been decidedly irreligious. And yet I found the idea of "doing a Lazarus"—for the crowned heads of Europe!—repugnant. But hadn't I, in my lifetime, done worse?

Far worse.

But still I could not bring myself to hand over the secret! Not for love or money.

We made the rounds of the local mediums and clairvoyants.

The wine glass moved. The table did a clog dance on the floor. The candles flickered and went out. Ethereal music and the smell of gardenias filled the darkened room. The table began to rise into the air.

Houdini jumped up, crying, "Fakery!"

Dressed as a woman, he exposed the concealed wires, the smoke and mirrors, the Victrola, and the perfumed sachet.

"I must know what is on the Other Side!" he shouted, tearing off his frumpy wig.

I offered to kill him, but he declined.

"Hold out your hands," he said, giving me an amusing wink.

I did so and before I knew it, he'd handcuffed me and put me in a trunk.

"There's a speaking tube by your mouth," he called from outside the trunk. "Tell me the secret and I'll dig you up at once."

And then he buried me!

Can you imagine the horror, listening to the gravel raining on the lid, the thudding clods of earth? Then nothing: silence. (If you cannot, ask a friend to bury you in the yard—then you'll know!)

"I can't remember!" I shouted through the speaking tube.

"Liar!" he shouted back in a distant, tinny voice.

But I had forgotten. In my panic, I could not remember a single Kikuyu syllable.

I screamed until I blacked out.

"I am not a murderer," Houdini said sadly.

We were sitting on camp stools, watching the elephants. He had uprooted me after my screams had abruptly ceased.

"Shall I tell you my greatest fear?" he asked after a long pause.

I shrugged indifferently. I confess I was not in the most charitable of moods. If I'd had my Winchester, I would have satisfied his
curiosity concerning the afterlife then and there.

"That death is irreversible; that there is no way back. I have
made a career of standing on the brink, but never once have I crossed
it."

"One day you will," I promised him with absolute assurance.

"And return to tell the tale?"

"Who knows?" I said.

I think now that if anyone can, surely it must be Houdini.

He rose and shook my hand warmly, begging my pardon for
having persecuted me. No more was said about the strange words
with the power to quicken. I was grateful: to make a present of the
form when the spirit is mean is folly. I believe he had resigned himself to the ineluctable end—the "tight spot" from which there can
be no wriggling, the final cabinet from which there is no escape.

But I may have been wrong.

As he climbed into his Voisin, he winked at me and said, "Who
knows? Perhaps it's not so bad after all."

He started his motor and in a moment his aeroplane escaped
earth and all of us who crawl, for a brief time, upon it. At least this
is how it seemed to me.

To stand at the brink takes courage, I thought later that night as
I readied myself for sleep, remembering with a shudder how I had
cowered there and screamed.

AFRICAN FOLLIES

Shortly after Houdini's disappointing visit to Africa, I contracted a mania for spiritualism. Although he had, during our tour of Mombasa mediums, regretfully exposed them one and all as fakes, I was by no means convinced of the impossibility of "piercing the veil."

You might well conclude that my ability to resuscitate the dead ought to settle the matter *ipso facto*; however, Pennington—with whom, it is true, I spoke posthumously, although with reluctance on his part—may not have been dead in the strict definition of the word, but rather an example of that *living* dead certain East African tribes are alleged to command. The old Kikuyu who instructed me in the dubious art of revival did not bother to clarify this—to my mind—significant point.

I resolved, therefore, to discover if contact with the Beyond could be made by other, less questionable means. I studied the literature, which is abundant if not always free of extravagant claims; took a correspondence course in mesmerism from the Society for Psychical Research; and built a special, windowless room whose purpose was to "entrap, induce, and oblige spiritual annunciations," according to the back issue of William Stainton Moses' *Light*, in which I found plans for a "spirit room."

I had been in the spirit room all morning, alternately dozing and mesmerizing myself in a shaving mirror, and had succeeded in conjuring only a small cloud. I was unhappy with the results, although the cloud appeared quite content in its new abode—so much so I would not have been surprised if it had mooed.

Suddenly, there was a knocking at the door. In hopes that it was an instance of "spirit-rapping," I opened the door at once but was disappointed to find Florenz Ziegfeld instead of a ghostly visitor standing outside.

"Do you know where I can find exotic women?" the Broadway impresario asked, taking off his high hat (not in deference to the sensitive precincts he had entered but rather in consideration of the ceiling whose height, for reasons known only to Mr. Moses, was specified at 5 foot, 3 inches exactly). "I'm looking for something different for this year's Follies," he said. "Frankly, I'm sick of 'glorifying the American Woman.'"

"Africa is filled with exotic women," I said, barely concealing my anger at his untimely intrusion. (In Africa, more than anyplace else on earth, people have a habit of dropping in unannounced.)

"I would pay well to find them," he said meaningfully.

I was on the point of remarking that I was no one's procurer when he asked, "Does this cloud belong to you?"

I told him it did, for who had a better claim?

"It would be fantastic on the stage of the New Amsterdam! The girls could wear it!"

I gave him a look he interpreted as puzzlement.

"To hide their pinkness in." He winked at me. "Just enough to escape a charge of indecency. It would be like a"—he felt around in the air a moment before finding the word he wanted—"*shimmering* organdy nightgown! I swear it would be a sensation."

I was offended, and perhaps it was to justify himself that he added, "Teddy Roosevelt attended my first Follies in '07 and pronounced it, 'Bully!'"

"The cloud," I said haughtily, "is not for sale."

"I am not the pantywaist you take me for," said Ziegfeld, as we rode through a forest of strange trees. "My life has been a rough-and-tumble one. I grew up in Chicago. I was a trick-shooter in Wyoming with Buffalo Bill's Wild West Show. I managed the world's strongest man. I have been shoved around and have shoved in my turn. Now that I am middle-aged and successful, I prefer the company of women."

"You've interrupted me at a crucial moment in my research!" I shouted in frustration.

"What research?"

"Spiritualism! I was trembling on the brink! I was close to it—to the chink in the wall through which I have only to put my hand to touch the dead!"

He laughed so hard he fell off his horse.

My face burned with shame!

"You know what the Secret of Life is?" asked Ziegfeld. "Sex."

"I'm not interested in life," I told him.

"An hour with one of my girls would change your mind."

He then did something appalling with his cigar.

I ran into the hills—desperate to get away from his lasciviousness. I am not, as any reader of these notes will confirm, prudish or misogynistic. I have loved women passionately. Sexual desire is as strong in me as in any other man. But the images Ziegfeld excited in me caused great perturbation and threatened to rout reason itself. The mere presence of the man was enough to make my head spin with fancies—never mind his "pinknesses" and "shimmering organdy nightgowns"! I had come to Africa, in part, to escape all that was lewd and dishonorable. (Yes, yes, I admit to fantasizing about Anna. And Mrs. Willoughby. But only in a way that does all of us credit.)

"What are you afraid of?" he shouted through a megaphone.

"Go back where you came from!" I screamed from the hilltop. "Africa has no need of you!"

"But the women—the auditions—the Follies! Why won't you help me?"

I squeezed myself into a hollowed-out tree and bit my tongue.

I left my hiding place and returned to the tents. I was hungry and thirsty—I am no saint, no desert ascetic crunching on locusts and licking up the morning dew!

"Spiritualism is a displacement of normal sexual desire," said Ziegfeld. "Instead of a living human being, you want to be possessed by a dead one, which, of course, is impossible—at least under ordinary circumstances."

I was about to object when he said (a little too smugly), "Dr. Freud is of the same opinion. I had the pleasure of an exchange of views in Mademoiselle Lillian's dressing room during his visit to New York. You see, like Africa, everyone sooner or later comes to the Follies."

"I assure you I am normal in every way," I said after swallowing a morsel of roasted elephant heart.

I locked myself in the spirit room.

Ziegfeld slid erotic playing cards under the door.

I concentrated my attention on the cloud.

"Such a nice cloud," I said.

The cloud nuzzled me gratefully.

Ziegfeld played "*Jardin de Paris*" through the door on the safari Victrola.

I stuffed my ears with bits of fleecy cloud and mesmerized myself. Then I unlocked the door and left the room.

Ziegfeld unstoppered my left ear and whispered something into it. Its power of suggestion was stronger than the hypnotic suggestion I had given myself, and I woke.

"Come with me," he said, taking me gently by the arm.

The girls stood under the trembling African sun, each wearing the blue blouse of a porter. Their skin was the color of burnished chestnuts, or amber, or ivory. Their hair—ebony, gold, or copper—astonished me with its radiance as if each strand were a light-bearing filament. They carried damascene cushions and silk umbrellas. They looked at me and smiled the secret smile of seduction.

"What do you say now?" asked Ziegfeld, without the slightest trace of malice.

I said nothing but already I felt myself in danger.

"Aren't they beautiful?" he said happily. "Aren't they better than anything the afterlife has to offer? And you don't have to die for them—you have only to want them."

"I'm looking at a mirage," I said, shaking my head hard to dispel it.

But it was not a mirage; it was an effect of the cloud that floated behind the girls, an immaterial backdrop for their shimmering.

My cloud!

Ziegfeld turned to them and nodded.

The girls lifted their dainty feet and began to kick to a music whose source I could not determine. With their pretty legs, they kicked at the supports of a structure which rose up in my mind like a shining city. The music played, and they kicked until the city wobbled and fell into a heap of broken images—each a mirror reflecting sun and sky and the green hills and the warm possibilities of flesh.

Ziegfeld saw in my eyes how I began to want the girls, and he laughed in pleasure and triumph. He saw in my mind how I picked up a brick and laid it in the chink between this world and the next, and he offered me a cigar.

"Pleasure is good," he said. "Desire is good. Life is meant to be lived on earth, not in some other place. The 'Beyond' is only the next minute you draw breath."

I thought, then, that I had misjudged him.

That night we set fire to the spirit room and watched it burn. The erotic playing cards and my back issues of *Light* were all consumed—transformed into a gorgeous shower of commingling, indistinguishable sparks.

Ziegfeld returned to America and his Follies. As for the girls, they vanished—whether onto the stage of the New Amsterdam Theatre or into the jungle to this day I do not know.

Africa is now a memory. As I spill gin on the board, inquiring of my Ouija whether tomorrow will be the day I meet someone who will lessen my loneliness—I wonder if those girls might not have been a mirage after all.

Ziegfeld laughs—from a stage in heaven or hell he is laughing at the follies of men, scattering his cigar ash like a *largesse*.

THE AERODYNAMICS OF DREAMS

He wanted to build a colossus, he said. A Wonder of the World. I reminded him that his tower was already so. His *Tour Eiffel* on the Champ-de-Mars. No, he said. Bigger. More lasting. It was more lasting fame he wanted now in his seventy-eighth year, and only a tower that would prove perpetual could ensure it. Iron, no matter how cunningly wrought, and masonry, no matter how expert, are not eternal. Especially here (he made a sweeping Gallic gesture that embraced Africa, the whole of it), where conditions conspire to frustrate the work of the hand. To thwart man's progress and bring down his monuments.

I poured him a tumbler of Bombay Gin—the Queen's own. He refused it, in his desperate resolve to create.

"You are too ambitious, Gustave," I reproached him.

(I had no ambition, as you well know. Have none now. I downed the Bombay and wiped my mustache with the back of my hand, theatrically, for this was theater, after all, and I had a part to play, even if a minor one.)

"Ambition in a man your age is ridiculous," I continued, enjoying his discomfiture.

"One can be only what one is," he shrugged. "From first to last." He took a notebook from his vest pocket and began to sketch. "I am an engineer."

Finished, he showed me his project. I stared at the page a moment—at the fine blue-veined graph paper (reminding me, strangely, of women's breasts), which was otherwise empty, his writing instrument having left no mark that I could see.

Reading my mind, he scoffed, "You can see nothing because you are a sot—a drunken oaf without imagination."

I was about to rise up in my indignation and beat him, but his twinkling eye forestalled me.

"It will be an *invisible* tower!" he cried triumphantly, so that the other customers in the Mombasa Hotel Bar looked up from their plates of roasted fowl. "I shall begin at once!"

"Not since Caruso have I encountered such an interesting case," said Freud, stroking his beard.

"It's all too obvious," I said.

"Nothing is obvious in psychiatry!" he chided.

"Nonsense, Sigmund!" I replied, meeting the gaze that flashed angrily round the edges of his wire-rims. "Eiffel is driven to erect a phallic symbol in subconscious protest against his approaching death.

Death takes no serious interest in life but sex represents a shameless challenge to its sovereignty," I hissed (because of the damned alliteration!). "Once sex is finished, life is easily extinguished. Intuiting this, Gustave heroically raises the flag."

(Years on Freud's couch had made me fluent in psychoanalytical flimflam.)

Freud grunted.

"But why should it be an invisible tower?" he asked.

"Because for an old man, sex is all in the head."

Freud laughed, appreciating a good joke.

At that moment, T. R. made an extraordinary entrance. His cowboy spurs clattered. The toy zebra ("Souvenir of Nairobi") whinnied. It was the former president throwing his voice from behind his heavy mustache. His flashing teeth and custom-tailored safari costume were splendid. (He, too, had a part to play.) He hated Freud and ignored him, introducing me to Colonel Goethals, who supervised the building of the Panama Canal. Out of office, Teddy had come to Africa with the Colonel to build a canal across the continent—"from the Indian Ocean to the Atlantic, a bully piece of engineering!"

Goethals laid his Panama hat on the bar and asked for a pitcher of water and a bucket of sand.

"To illustrate a fundamental principle of hydrology."

"Bully!"

I was surrounded by madmen.

Eiffel stood in a clearing a day's walk from Mombasa. He stood erect with his legs wide apart: a great, inverted V of determination. It moved me. It was as if he were standing on the Champ-de-Mars, transmogrified into the tower. I could almost see the tourists swarming under his hat, peering out at Paris through tiny holes in his hatband. Golden weaver birds flew twittering about him. I was, as I said, moved by the sight: an old man, dreaming himself into the future, rooted in his past, indifferent to Africa's hot, cobalt sky.

"How goes it?" I said, taking his arm in friendship.

"It rises," he said happily. "Each day another flight. Soon dirigibles will moor at the top—dirigibles sailing over the oceans to Africa."

"Yes," I said to humor him.

(Why not? He was no threat to me. Besides, I may have loved him at that moment.)

I gave him a sandwich. He sat on the grass and unwrapped the oiled paper. The sun glistened in its crinkles. The sandwich paper was as minutely lined as his face. I felt a tenderness for him. I remembered my father, who had never left Cincinnati. I tried to compose in my mind a tribute to my father but could not; the words would not come to me. I left my father to his earth in Cincinnati and sat with Gustave, on into the gathering African dusk, silent, feeling a migration of earthworms beneath me as a new Eiffel Tower ascended above the African plain, and also descended, for even imaginary towers must be grounded in bedrock.

It was, as I remember at this remove in time and space (myself become an old man retired to a room in Cincinnati)—it was a *poetic* moment. I was glad Freud was not with me: for him, poetry was merely another aspect of the unconscious mind, susceptible to analysis; and I was in no mood for disillusionment—so rare were moments of exultation, so rare rapture.

"I met Apollinaire once," said Eiffel as we watched a pink string of flamingos stretch across the wide, setting sun. "He was sitting in a cafe, looking at my tower. He had made a drawing of it on a piece of paper. I invited to show him the original—point out the secrets of its construction. He shook his head. 'No thank you, *monsieur*,' he said. 'I have comprehended it.' Then he showed me his drawing. This."

Eiffel took a piece of paper from his wallet and carefully unfolded it.

"A calligram, he called it."

There on the paper an Eiffel Tower dissolved before my eyes into a black drizzle of letters of the alphabet. Rogue punctuation marks. As I stared in bewilderment, a comma hopped off the page.

"A flea," Eiffel smiled and folded up the paper. "Apollinaire was right. The poet is the true engineer, and he does not have to see the original to comprehend its secrets—only to imagine it."

Madness!

In the Mombasa Hotel, Wilbur and Orville were looking for Eiffel.

"We've read his essay on aeronautics: 'The Resistance of Air.' It interests us profoundly. There are one or two points we would like him to clarify," they said as one, for they were not only inseparable but indistinguishable.

"He is sleeping," I told them.

"Ah!" they said, taking off their derbies in respect. The brothers knew that in sleep, in dreams, the mathematics of flight is, little by little, elaborated.

They glanced reverentially upwards where, in a second-floor bedroom, Eiffel lay sleeping and, beyond, toward the beckoning sky.

"We will come back later," Wilbur and Orville said, putting on their derbies as one in a gesture of perfect fraternity.

Outside in the dusty street, the brothers got into their aeroplane, started the motor, and jumped into the sky, which opened to receive them. The machine became a dot in the blue Mombasa air before vanishing altogether to an *adagio* for strings.

In the room over my head, Eiffel had risen from his bed and hovered close to the ceiling—or so the pretty *femme de chambre* swore to me later when I took her in my arms to attempt a flight of another sort entirely.

Teddy and the Colonel labored long at their canal under the terrible African sun. I thought it an impossible scheme, although it caused Mrs. Willoughby's husband, who managed the Uganda railroad, many sleepless nights. Suffering from an insomnia all my own, I dallied with the *femme de chambre*; and while she may have lacked the mature charms of a Mrs. Willoughby, she was content (in the way of young girls) to play the shepherd's game by the moonlit Indian Ocean. She needed neither *soirées* nor De Beers to make her happy.

The Wright brothers did not return, having—it was rumored— crashed into the sea because of an accumulation of comet dust on the fragile wings of their machine.

It turned out to be otherwise. They had flown to Paris and let their heads be turned by the *Folies-Bergères*. But only for a brief time—outside of history so to speak, inside a history of the imagination where Apollinaire and Jarry, Rousseau and Satie are always strolling the streets of Montmartre. Before war came and killed everything.

"You are imagining things," Freud muttered from a shadowy corner of his darkened consulting room.

I was once more in therapy because the old anxiety had returned. I had the power to see the future. Not always, but from time to time it visited me: the truth—unlike the faked messages from the panders of the otherworld Houdini, dressed as a woman, had unmasked during Mombasa *séances*. And the future made me anxious, made me shake so that I could scarcely raise the gin glass to my lips! Shall I tell you what I saw in those awful moments of clairvoyance?

"Shall I tell you what's coming, Sigmund?"

"The Talking Cure is highly efficacious," he nodded.

"What's coming is this: Poison gas clouds cruelly fragrant with apples and almonds. Night, slowly falling flares, and the light on the wire almost beautiful. Bodies blooming on the wire, in the mangled valley and the flooded trench—the trench from whose filthy lips men are birthed into history and death. Shell-shocked hysterics dancing to an unstoppable jazz *macabre*. Men, their pockets full of water, rocking in the fire-swept ocean. Aeroplanes loosed from dreams of desire into the bloody air that strums dirges on their wing-wires. And more—much more concealed in the terror-struck mind's ellipsis…"

"You are injuring yourself past fixing," said Freud, when I'd finished raving. "This poetry mysteriously afflicting you is a plague, is pathological, is whispered to you from a sick brain—yours. If you're not careful, you'll end up a victim of your own death wish."

Teddy Roosevelt: "It's the fault of Halley's comet that so many of us have lost our minds."

Colonel Goethals: "We dig so as not to know we are already dead men, though what we dig is our grave."

Sigmund Freud: "In dreams we fly unassisted because of the strength of our desire to penetrate the sky, the universe, other bodies."

Gustave Eiffel: "The aerodynamics of dreams is perfect. The dreamer ascends without wings, without any other means of propulsion than his own wish to escape the earth, which is a grave. A mulch pit."

"I want to make a present of my newest principle—'The Aerodynamics of Dreams'—to Wilbur and Orville so that they can leave history and become myth."

We were on the building site outside Mombasa. Eiffel assured me that his tower was nearly finished, though I could see it only indistinctly and in some lights. Twilight seemed the most favorable. At that hour the light slashed and shadows made what was least visible, visible. Each blade of grass etched itself onto the field of vision. In the case of an invisible object, however, patience is required. Patience and imagination, which I hoped to inflame with the help of my pocket flask.

"It would be tragic if aeroplanes were to be exploited by entrepreneurs," Eiffel continued. "They are better left as metaphors."

"Wilbur and Orville have left Africa for good," I said.

"No matter. I will send them my treatise by wire."

"The telegraph wire was brought down by a stampeding herd of giraffes."

"Is the dream-wire still intact?"

I was about to answer when Teddy and Colonel Goethals floated by on a canal barge.

"We are making bully progress!" they shouted.

The gramophone played on deck and I could not separate in my mind the music that fell, note by note, onto the coppery river and the flakes of light shaken out by the setting sun.

"Is it real?" I asked Eiffel, having learned in Africa to mistrust the evidence of my senses. "The boat, the canal—T. R. and the Colonel crooning a song about the Mountains of the Moon?"

Eiffel was unable to speak, choked by profound emotion.

"*Surreal*," said Apollinaire, who had just debarked from a dirigible moored by the dream-wire to the top of Eiffel's tower. In the swiftly falling night I saw it clearly now. Because of the lights strung across the observation deck railings. Saw the dirigible, too—a shining thought.

"It is beautiful," I said, finding myself again moved.

"It is a dream," said Apollinaire.

"It is a dream turned inside out to become life," said Eiffel.

The Eiffel Tower glittered in the blackness of night—a monument to the imagination, which is lasting. To poetry and engineering. And to Gustave, who combined both brilliantly in a single invention.

The gramophone played.

The barge rustled among stiff reeds.

The burnished river soughed.

The dirigible mooed.

All was beautiful!

Hand in hand, Eiffel and I ascended the tower.

THE BOOK OF CASUALTIES

He was sad, he said. "*Triste.*" I was moved—by his sadness and that he should tell me it in French, a language he mistrusted. I touched his shoulder, tentatively, in case he should misunderstand. "*Triste,*" he repeated.

"What is your sorrow?" I asked, replenishing his drink.

"I have lost my place in history," he said.

"You've had a brilliant career," I replied, wanting to console him.

"I have had my crowded hour."

I tapped on the window for Kermit. He was outside in the street, dealing with the askari policemen, who were demanding bribes.

Kermit paid them off and came into the barroom.

I indicated his father, who was slumped over a plate of small, roasted birds.

"What is wrong?" Kermit asked, removing his hat.

"He is in despair," I told him. "Over his place in history."

"Damn the fat man!" he snarled, alluding to Taft, who had succeeded T. R. as President in 1908.

"I told him his place is secure," I said.

"Father…"

Kermit laid his hand on Teddy's. I was again moved—this time by the young man's tenderness.

"He will feel better once he's killed something," I promised.

"How am I to be remembered?" cried Teddy, his anguished voice muffled in his arms.

We bore the former President into the jungle. He was listless, indifferent—refusing all food and drink. His head wobbled inside the palanquin that rested on the broad, black shoulders of the porters. The flag, which he had brought from America to decorate his triumphs in the bush, was drawn up under his chin.

"My shroud," he said in a small voice. "The red, white, and blue."

I laughed, hoping to revive his famous good humor.

"Black Care has caught up with me at last," he said plaintively.

His son Kermit brought him a roasted elephant heart to "put the iron back in the old man"; but Teddy would have none of it, preferring—he said—to remember "better days." And then, as if to put himself in a fitting frame of mind, he rolled from the palanquin into a ditch.

This proved too much for Kermit. It was—he would later say—as if a national monument, a sacred instrument, a *faith* had been besmirched by the African dust. He tossed his portion of elephant heart (an excellent tidbit, by the way, which I greatly miss)—tossed his morsel into the bush and ran away so that we might not witness his grief at the wreck of his once mighty father.

"I have lost my bully pulpit," mourned Teddy.

Onward.

Teddy carried by the porters.

Past the last outposts, hoping to leave his Black Care behind.

Teddy once again in the ditch. This time because of a defection of porters who had left him there unceremoniously while our eyes were closed.

The palanquin taken up by Carlson and Captain Slade.

The journey resumed. Halted.

Our encampment on the banks of the Guaso Nyero where Georges Méliès had transfigured the African night with Halley's comet and his cinematic art.

Strange cries offstage.

Trompe l'oeil shadows.

The beating of invisible wings.

The impenetrable wilderness, which we, nevertheless, were penetrating with each step forward. (Or perhaps the wilderness parted like the Red Sea of old in order to drown us unawares in midstep!)

Sudden fear followed by fervent prayers to Yahweh, Jehovah, Allah, and savage household gods.

A rumor of war reaching us even here, from time blown backward on the wind of history (which is usually at our backs but had somehow gotten ahead of us).

"Send the gunboats; the Hun is massing!" Teddy shouted in his delirium.

(But who in 1912 was listening?)

"My dear Mr. President!"

Dale Carnegie was in Africa, exercising the power of positive thinking.

"My dear Mr. President!" he repeated, pressing a yellow pamphlet into his hands.

"What do you want here?" I asked gruffly, having taken an instant dislike to him.

"I wish to make a present of my enthusiasm."

While enthusiasm was certainly in short supply, I didn't care to accept his and told him to keep it. There was something unctuous in his manner that put me in mind of hair oil.

He took no offense. He smiled, handed me a tract, and withdrew into the—as yet—tractless wilderness to make friends and influence the indigenous people there. Secretly, I hoped they would persuade him into one of their large cooking pots—the type reserved for officious missionaries for which Africa is famous.

"The century will belong to men like him," said Kermit, who had returned to our little expedition with his grief in check. "To salesmen."

As if on cue, a hyena laughed mockingly.

"Care for a cigarette?" I asked, holding out my packet of Abdullas.

Kermit accepted one with extreme cordiality, and we passed a pleasant quarter of an hour discharging our rifles at small mammals.

His ague having spent itself, Teddy slept, covered with the flag whose stars looked fine against the gloomy jungle backdrop.

"Your father belongs to a more heroic age," I said.

Kermit nodded.

"It would have been better if he had died leading the charge up San Juan Hill," I said, "rather than come to this."

"His war was cut short by a too-quickly sued-for peace," said Kermit.

"The Spanish were certainly a disappointment," I agreed.

"Perhaps the Germans will oblige him with a war worthy of the name."

(Had he, too, heard the rumor?)

"Worthy of *him*!" I asservated.

(They would not. Alas, it was to be that *Princetonian's* war—"Mr. Wilson's War," not Roosevelt's. Teddy would miss the boat for this, the bloodiest century in history.)

"It's getting dark," Kermit observed.

"We are close to the heart," I said. "The heart of the Dark Continent."

"Alice!" cried Teddy.

We entered the darkness at a little past 6 o'clock (AM or PM—it was impossible to tell). Immediately, we were met with "*Semper Fidelis*," clamorous in the immaculate silence of the wilderness at dead center.

I detested military marches, but for Teddy's sake did nothing that would spoil his triumphal entry.

The music grew to the verge of the lines that imprison it, went a step or two beyond, then fell silent as the last notes decayed into the immensity.

We helped Teddy onto a recently constructed bandstand. Sweeping away excelsior, I recalled the surveyor's words at the beginning of my journey: "He will come once the country is safe." How little he knew Sousa! The country was far from safe but here was the March King in his natty dress uniform and mustache, tucking his baton under his arm to acknowledge Kermit's applause.

"Bravo!" I called, for form's sake.

"What's happened to Teddy? Has he been gored?" Sousa inquired, after saluting his former Commander-in-Chief.

"He has lost his bully pulpit," I said.

"It is the nation's loss," Sousa remarked, bowing his head. "And the fat man?" he inquired, meaning Taft.

"Flourishing," I said.

Kermit spat his contempt into the bush.

"Where is the band?" I asked, looking around me for the first time and seeing no one else. "Where are the instrumentalists?"

"Hiding," Sousa answered. "Behind the trees. They are afraid of the coming war."

Teddy roused himself from his neurasthenic "vapors" and shouted, "Charge!"

But the Rough Riders were in America, growing old; and in the war to come, men would dig inside the earth or drown under a green-gas sea.

"Alice!" cried Teddy.

"Who is Alice?" Freud asked.

"His first wife," said Kermit—"died soon after giving birth to my half-sister."

"Pity," said Freud.

"Can you put his troubled mind at rest?" asked Kermit, anxiety causing his ordinarily steady voice to break.

"Not here. He must visit me in my Mombasa office on Queen Victoria Street. My leather couch is there, in the room behind the always shuttered blinds, on a Persian rug chosen especially for its convoluted design."

"What brings you so far from Mombasa's pleasant streets and sea air to the dark and pestilential heart of Africa?" I asked.

"A dream," he replied wistfully. "It is always so."

The dead man, Pennington, stepped out from behind a juniper tree. I thought of Hamlet's "too, too solid flesh." Despite my former friend's moonlit face, there was no lightness to his movements; rather, he seemed to bear upon him the heaviness of matter as if some undiscovered element had settled in him, as if an extreme form of gravity held him to the earth.

I took a step towards him, but Freud stayed me with his hand.

"A dream," he repeated; and seeing the tears start up in his eyes, I was afraid. "A dream of death."

"Alice!" cried Teddy.

"Bring him to Queen Victoria Street," said Freud, presenting Kermit with a black-edged card.

"And my friend?" I asked, nodding towards Pennington.

"I can do nothing for him," Freud answered sadly. "He is in love."

Teddy slept.

Kermit slept.

Carlson and Captain Slade slept.

The porters, whom we had suffered to return, put down their burdens and slept. It was not the sleeping sickness; it was something else—a profound weariness, like a hand upon the heart.

Freud hunted for Thanatos among the trees. In the black water. Among the fever ticks. He hunted for death in order to understand its seductiveness. Its fascination. Its irresistible beauty. Already he was learning that death, not desire, lies behind all things visible and invisible. That it is death that men love, although he will suppress this knowledge for years to come.

"Anna!" I shouted into the stillness.

The stillness broke like a piece of glass.

Anna was asleep in the Hamptons. She did not know me anymore.

I could not sleep.

I walked farther still. *Further* still, into time. The wind shrieked inside me; the rain drizzled through the tree of my blood. The starry night was an x-ray film showing the sickness of the world. Marie Curie dazzled by radium computed the arithmetic of decay on the abacus of her bones. Box cars heavy with wretchedness rolled towards smoking towers. Albert, whom I had once guided through the impossibilities of Africa, covered his bare head under a strange rain. The dead who had died in the century that was to come tugged at my sleeves.

I tried to cry out a human name, but my mouth was stoppered up against me.

It was then I found *The Book of Casualties*. Who kept it, in whose neat hand the entries had been painstakingly recorded—I cannot tell. I never saw the bookkeeper, only the book. Its pages were lead, the entries in red grease pencil. History, it seemed to say, is cold and indestructible; men, an impermanent mark of rent flesh and spent blood.

I read a while in the history of slaughter. In panic I hunted for my name among the lost but the names were all of places unknown to me: Verdun, the Somme, Passchendaele, Anatolia, Guernica, Auschwitz, Babi Yar, Hiroshima…each followed by a number whose magnitude abolished the very idea of a single human life.

I tried to close the heavy book, but it would not close.

At the end of history is a small stage. The curtain is drawn; the house lights are turned off. Happy to rest, I sat down in the empty theater and waited. I thought how nice it would be if Anna were here…or Mrs. Willoughby. I slept. And woke. And thought I ought to look behind the curtain. What I saw there must be instructive; at the very least it would give me something intelligent to contribute to the cocktail conversation at the Mombasa Club (I, who am usually so silent and embarrassed), or reconcile Albert to Africa with an explanation for its unsettling roguishness that would satisfy his demand for a unified theory. You owe it to yourself to investigate, I told myself—now that you're here, after coming such a long way. But I was suddenly indifferent to what might lie behind the curtain. A lassitude such as I have seldom experienced possessed me. I cannot explain it: I had only to get out of my seat, walk a few steps down the aisle—past the pit—reach out and twitch the curtain aside. But I hadn't the strength. Or the curiosity, despite the music coming from the other side, which sounded like a Sigmund Romberg operetta. It was easier to sit and do nothing and be glad I was alone.

I had gone as far as I could go. It wasn't weariness or apathy that stayed me now (I had revived after leaving the theater), but a lack of options: there was no *place*, not even an impenetrable one, in which to continue the journey. I had come up against an intractability. A coagulation of matter. A goo. I searched for a door, but there was none.

I turned and started back. The return journey unwound at unholy speed so that only blurred and jittery images of what had gone before were apparent:

The terrible book.

The strange rain.

Marie Curie glowing in the dark like a watch dial.

The shattered stillness reglazed.

Freud among the trees.

The expedition asleep.

The bandstand deconstructing, the excelsior flying back into the board.

Carnegie's nauseous enthusiasm.

Rumors of war become screams.

Teddy in the ditch.

An advertisement for Vinolia Otto Toilet Soap, soap of choice aboard R.M.S. *Titanic*—"Standard of Toilet Luxury and Comfort at Sea"—which had blown out of someone else's history and fallen like a wind-tossed newspaper into mine.

Teddy slumped over a plate of roasted birds.

Kermit arguing with the askaris in the street.

Back further and farther until once more I stood on the shore of Lake No with Ross, irresolute, afraid to cross, wishing I were home in the Hamptons with Anna or, better still, outside history, the grim history, the terrible history—a boy in Cincinnati, dreaming of Africa.

And then—forward, into the future. For who is there to prevent it?

"It is not possible," he said.

"Why not?" I asked.

We were drinking martinis in a bar at the top of the Empire State Building: Merian Cooper, Fay Wray, and a morose, dark-set man who was playing the part of King Kong. He suffered "cruelly," he said, from the weight and heat of the ape costume. Cooper threw a cocktail spear at him. "Whine! Whine! Whine!" he said mockingly. The man, whose name I never caught, scratched himself incessantly "because of the goddamn fleas!" and drank, as Fay put it, "rather more than is good for him."

"Why not?" I repeated.

Cooper had hired me as his technical advisor on *King Kong* because of my long years as an "Africa hand." I had just finished relating my trek to the end of history and suggested a scene be shot there—"to attract the highbrows."

"You cannot film under such conditions," said Cooper.

"Méliès pulled it off in '10!'"

"Méliès was not a realist!" Cooper replied heatedly.

"And you are?" I sneered. "I knew Kong in the old days and yours"—with a contemptuous glance at the flea-bitten stand-in—"is nothing like him!"

The director turned serious.

"Kong is dangerous; I won't have him on the set!" he said. "And what you propose is also dangerous. Méliès stopped at the Guaso Nyero whereas you propose leading us right smack into a goo! The underwriters would never stand for it."

Fay interjected, "Tell me about Mrs. Willoughby."

"Later," I promised, feeling the first faint stirrings of desire.

"Impossible," the director concluded.

"I know the way!" I argued (no longer sure that I did).

I wanted to return to the end of history—to the stage whose curtain I had failed to part. For twenty-one years I had been dying to know what lies behind it. I hadn't the courage to go alone, nor, in middle-age, the strength. My curiosity was to remain unsatisfied.

"We stick to the shooting schedule," Cooper growled. "If it can't be storyboarded, we ain't filming it!"

We stood at the window of her apartment and watched the lights tremble on the East River. Night pressed against the window. Shadows oiled the floor. Sigmund Romberg's *The Desert Song* played on the gramophone. Fay turned her head and looked at the Empire State Building rising into the sky—stars confused with the lights of its upper stories.

"It's like a gigantic penis—isn't it?" she said nervously.

I blushed profoundly.

"I would ask Freud, but we're no longer on speaking terms," I said.

"I'm afraid," she whispered.

"Of Kong?"

"No, of the Empire State Building. Merian won't use a double even though he knows I'm scared to death of heights."

"It's all about death," I said, gulping my gin. "Even sex is about death."

Fay shivered, and I took her in my arms, awkwardly because of the gin. Conscious of her slim body through the crepe of her dress, I was aroused as of old. The gramophone had not yet wound down; *The Desert Song* played softly. I wondered at the long and tortuous path that had led me to Fay's apartment, at my own history which had not yet ended, and of the casualties that were not written down in any book. Then I thought of the sweetness of the woman in my arms, there if only for this one evening.

I sniffed her perfumed neck as I had once seen Kong do to Mrs. Willoughby's and was suddenly afraid.

"Beauty atones for the long death," I whispered and almost believed it as I caught sight of a dark shape crouched outside the window.

HUNTING ICEBERGS

Sousa stood on the shore of Lake Victoria, sobbing into his sousaphone. It was a mournful sight, and we closed our hampers uncomfortably. We had left Entebbe early that morning for a *fête champêtre* and had not heard the news. Then the message arrived, delivered by hand, "From a Friend."

The *Titanic* had been lost—that strong ship—"scratched by an iceberg."

"It's wrong to eat our sandwiches and play the shepherd's game," I said, wondering what friend had sent the message and how he had known where to find me.

She nodded solemnly and did up her ribbons.

"Icebergs should be hunted to extinction!" she said earnestly. "All the big-game hunters should leave Africa at once for the North Atlantic."

She fell down on the reed mat and wept for the watery death of so many.

I knew I ought to volunteer to lead a safari to hunt the icebergs. She wanted it and, failing to act, I would dim in her eyes (so lovely, so brown!). But I hadn't the strength for such an undertaking. It was all I could do to fall asleep each night and then, each morning, wake.

Sousa ceased and entered the hatch of a submarine. We heard the bell ring on deck, and then the submarine slid smoothly into the depths of the lake.

"He is going to play a dirge at sea," she said.

But this was mere conjecture, and I doubted whether one could reach the ocean from the interior of Africa in a submarine.

"Unless there is a subterranean passage," she said. "An underground river is well within the realm of possibility."

I thought this was nonsense but kept my own counsel. I had high hopes of resuming the shepherd's game after a suitable period of mourning. I touched her white shoulder in an ambiguous gesture of sympathy or seduction.

"Thank you," she said.

We gathered our sandwich papers, rolled up the reed mat, and returned to Entebbe, our thoughts on the sea.

That night I dreamed I was with him—with Sousa, on the submarine. Because it looked like a sousaphone, I was not at all surprised to hear a lovely underwater passage.

It sounded like this in the lower register: *Ooooommmm!*

"What you hear is whales singing each to each," she said in my dream.

"No, it is Sousa's submarine in the lower register," I insisted.

(In the upper register, it skirled.)

"You are only guessing," she said in her shepherdess' blouse.

I looked out the window at the walls of the underground river. Here and there a mirror gave me back my own face, which was flushed because of my nearly overmastering desire to undo the ribbons on her blouse.

(No, I'm sorry, but I will not tell you her name. She has become a famous missionary in Africa. I'll mention the fish instead: they were brightly tropical and then, quite suddenly, gray as we entered the North Atlantic channel.)

"What is the water temperature?" she asked.

I looked at the thermometer riveted to the outside of the hull.

"37° Fahrenheit."

"What is that in centigrade?" she asked.

"I don't know!" I said, much annoyed.

"Why were you so annoyed?" she asked the following morning, over buttered toast.

We had agreed to tell each other our dreams, no matter how unkindly we had acted toward each other in them.

"I don't know," I said, truly.

Out on the North Atlantic, the icebergs drifted willy-nilly into the shipping lanes.

"Do they do it deliberately?" she asked as we played the shepherd's game under the mosquito net.

The Entebbe night was sultry, but I shivered at the thought of malevolent icebergs—icebergs with navigation and decision-making ability.

"Icebergs are the elephants of the ocean," I said, changing the subject.

"I feel immortal under the mosquito net," she said, laughing. She was pink (mostly).

"What did he say?" she demanded. "What did *Sousa* say?"

I knew she was referring to my dream of two nights before, but I pretended perversely not to understand.

Now it was her turn to be annoyed.

"In your dream!" she shouted.

"He locked himself in his cabin," I said. "I never got the chance to sound him."

She sighed.

"What an opportunity you missed there!"

"Why didn't you speak to him yourself then?" I asked hotly.

"It wasn't my dream," she answered with a flounce.

Just then Carlson, Hanby, and Blunt—friends with whom I had lost contact after the Mombasa mischief—entered with their double-barreled Hollands bristling.

"We're going to hunt down the iceberg that destroyed the *Titanic*!" they shouted. "And any other icebergs that get in our way."

She rose from the table and left the room. She said nothing, but I knew she was crying as she did up her ribbons.

"You've become effeminate," they said. "Take off that ridiculous costume and come with us!"

I measured them each out a gin while I considered my response.

"Have you studied the matter?" I asked, after a long pause filled with the appreciative sounds of their drinking.

"What matter?" they asked.

"How best to kill an iceberg. Where its vitals lie."

"No, but we shall practice on the smaller ones we meet on the way."

"I am with you then," I said.

They hoorayed me thrice.

"A kiss goodbye?" I called through the bedroom door. But she would not come out, neither would she answer.

"Are we traveling by submarine?" I asked as we dawdled in the yard to take our bearings.

"What an idea!" they hooted. "We're going by steamer."

They snapped their compasses shut and pointed toward Tunis.

"That way," they said.

Icebergs are much taller than I imagined, and their color is more blue than gray (in some lights, rosy). They do not look much like elephants.

"I was wrong: icebergs are not the elephants of the ocean," I wrote her. "I am not yet sure what they are; but when I know, I will write you again. Love from your devoted Shepherd."

I posted the letter, then went up on deck to stand watch.

Carlson, Hanby, and Blunt were asleep!

I whisked the snow from them and shook them roughly awake.

"Derelicts!" I shouted. "Slackers!"

They shrugged sheepishly.

"Our eyes grew heavy," they said. "We could not hold out a moment's longer against sleep."

I tied bells around them so that, should they drift off again, I would hear of it.

Ding! went a practice ring.

I adjusted the timbre setting.

Dong!

"Better," I said, satisfied.

We have entered a field of icebergs. So extraordinary are they that I find myself forgetting their homicidal nature. They rise from the iron sea like blue-gray buildings. One recalls a wintry New York or Paris just before rain, except that these buildings move—slowly, but oh, how majestically! When the sun flashes on them, they are most beautiful. But their beauty is lethal. I must not forget this!

The bells ring constantly as Carlson, Hanby, and Blunt sink under the weight of sleep. There is something in the air intensely soporific. Not the cold, but a dreaminess. Let them sleep! I do not want to share this scene with anyone.

Carlson, Hanby, and Blunt are fast asleep, under a shroud of snow. Their Hollands poke out like rusty spokes. I am the sole consciousness of this immense northern ocean.

Unless the icebergs are conscious!

The icebergs are waltzing!

Help!

No, I am in no danger. They glide together over the frozen ocean's polished floor. Blue and rose dancers. I would dance, too, but I'm afraid to shame myself in front of these graceful waltzers.

If only she were here, or Anna, who lived with me for a time in Wilbur and Orville's bicycle shop. But they are fading, their faces—crowded out of my mind's eye by the icebergs.

Sousa stands on the deck of the submarine, waving his baton. I wish he would go—and he does! He climbs down the hatch (I hear his shoes ring on the metal rungs) and the ship dives under an ice sheet.

I'm alone with them.

I love the icebergs!

I was undressing when Carlson, Hanby, and Blunt woke. They seized me in time to prevent my jumping overboard. I wanted to make love to the icebergs. I was prepared to die in their embrace.

"Steady on!" they said. "Icebergs are no friend to man. Remember the *Titanic*."

They locked me in the engine room where the cherry-red steam boiler soon had my blood flowing at 98.6° Fahrenheit. (I don't know what that is in centigrade.) They did not unlock the door until we bumped up against Tunis.

"Africa!" they said, excitedly, as we stood on deck.

How blue the sea is! How lovely the junipers!

We left the ship without a backward glance at the horizon, beyond which the terrible icebergs do a dance of death to the rattling bones of the drowned. As we strolled through the forest of green monkeys, we soon forgot all about those cold-blooded assassins.

What had I seen in them to love?

And then I smiled secretly at the thought of her, fragrant under the mosquito net.

"What are you smiling at?" Carlson, Hanby, and Blunt asked, one after the other.

"Nothing."

I found her sighing in a thicket of dreams. I touched her breast; she woke and pulled my hand away.

"Your hand is cold!" she said, angry for having been so rudely wakened.

"My love—"

"You should have stayed with your icebergs!"

Her reproach hung in the air between us, insubstantial yet impenetrable, like the mosquito net behind which she cowered.

"I went for you. I wore your pink ribbon round my neck."

I showed her it.

"To avenge the great ship!"

"Your hand is cold," she whined. "Go away."

I went out into the yard. The hot Entebbe night withdrew. The insect voices stilled to a winter modality. And in the stillness I heard them sing—heard the icebergs sing to me from the distant, freezing waves.

I prayed for Sousa, for his blaring band to come and drown their song; but it did not come.

Oh, you sirens!

A DISCOURSE ON HISTORY

When the Bishop entered my dreams, I had to kill him. Surely you can understand that! Consider how he dogged me through the streets of Mombasa, howling anathemas after me for my "licentiousness." He was referring to my shameless pursuit of Mrs. Willoughby, whose charming house on Prince Albert Street drew me, as it had drawn Kong to her very bed. Mrs. Willoughby fascinated many who found themselves in Africa. It was she who introduced me to her sometime lover, Vladimir Ilich Lenin. The two "Siggies"—Freud and Romberg—were once frequent visitors to Prince Albert Street, as much to view the voluptuous Mrs. Willoughby as to sip champagne cocktails on her veranda. Near the end of his life, Henry James had paid his respects to the lady, contriving to purloin one of her gloves "in remembrance." Mombasa was, in 1912, the place to be when in Africa; and Mrs. Willoughby's was the destination for the cultured and the curious. That Mr. Willoughby was, more often than not, absent from Prince Albert Street supplied a noticeable *frisson* to our visits.

The Bishop took it much amiss. Ever vigilant against breaches of public decency, he would stand by the hour behind the drapery or in the hallway outside Mrs. Willoughby's bedroom with his jaundiced eye screwed to the keyhole. We were constantly tripping over his crosier as we passed to and fro. Leave your crosier in the vestibule umbrella stand! we shouted, and received only curses for our pains.

"I would bar you and your sort from this house, had I the power," he growled. "Unhappily, Kenya is not a theocracy. Were it, I would devise ingenious punishments to chasten you."

The Bishop was a prig, and we told him so at every opportunity, giving him an occasional thumping for emphasis.

"Swine!" he would mutter as he straightened his ecclesiastical high hat knocked askew by our violent attack on his dignity. "Adulterers!"

I remember one evening on Prince Albert Street in particular: we were on the veranda, toasting Mrs. Willoughby's return and watching the sun die among the minarets. To the east the ocean heaved itself up, then flattened with a hiss as the light went out of the sky. I assured Mrs. Willoughby that the sun would rise again, after the usual adjournment—*there* (pointing oceanward); but she was unconvinced, having acquired in Africa a skepticism that a richly varied experience had only confirmed. "Perhaps," she said and sighed, taking my proffered hand. The "Pineapple Rag" drifted through the French windows, pausing on the veranda as if to quicken her mood, then blew beyond the railings and the topiary like a sheet of windswept rain to the sea. We were talking about the Special Theory of Relativity. The year before, Albert had arrived in Africa, wanting to forget—Mileva, his wife; his carping colleagues at the University of Zürich ("Mister Negatives!" he called them); and the terrible anxieties of four-dimensional existence. I had taken him on safari through the interior to distract him with the flora and fauna of Africa, but it had not been a success.

The music stopped abruptly, and Scott brought a stranger onto the veranda and, after putting a drink in his hand and introducing him as none other than H. G. Wells, went inside to resume his playing. Ragtime had but little time left before war and jazz finished it forever, and Joplin wished to make the most of it.

"What brings you to Mombasa?" I asked Wells, whom I hated on sight because of the sexual energy he radiated in the vicinity of the Object of My Desire, whose amorous gaze now rested on the Great Man.

"Mrs. Willoughby," he answered, lifting her hand to his lips. "Lady, your fame has jumped the ocean—and deservedly so," he said, kissing it (her hand, that is).

She was pleased.

I took him aside and admonished him: "She is mine."

"Are you a *sultan*?" he asked scornfully. "Women belong to no one but themselves."

"Suffragette!" I hissed. "Shavian!"

He laughed unpleasantly in my face. I shoved him, and he tripped over his valise. A sheaf of papers spilled across the flagstones of the path that led to the belvedere above the Indian Ocean.

"What is that?" I asked, as the wind winnowed the manuscript pages.

"My history!" he cried, playing hopscotch on the tumbling papers, whitely luminous under the moon, in an effort to save them from joining "The Pineapple Rag" scattering, note by note, on the water. "For God's sake, man—can't you help me!"

I helped him, though I hated him.

"Thank you," he said, as he shut up the papers in his valise.

We were sitting in the belvedere. The lights of an unseen steamer shivered against the blackness. I studied Wells' face in the sidereal light and thought it ordinary.

"I, too, am writing a history: *A History of the Imagination*."

"What's in it?" he asked.

"Everything that is not in yours," I taunted him.

"Then it's a lie!" he said with a vehemence I thought extreme.

I retaliated: "Mine is a history of *possibilities…*"

"I do not understand you."

I pointed to the steamer which by now had entered the bay.

"The boat will sink, or not—depending," I said. "You write the history that lies in its wake while I write of its possible encounters with the unknown. In this, mine is a history of the future. Like your *Time Machine* or *War of the Worlds*."

Wells stopped his pacing of the narrow enclosure to shout his indignation at me: "They are fictions!"

"But no less real for their being so."

"You're a lunatic!"

"Time is richer than you suppose," I said. "You imagine it as a succession of singular moments like a string of pearls. I see it as…"—I hunted for a suitable image with which to convey the dizzying complexity of time and settled on the firmament—"as the night sky with its countless stars."

He beat the air with his fists in a perfect fury.

"I have not come all this way to listen to your ravings! I've come to seduce Mrs. Willoughby. As I have seen the lady for myself, I know she is not a product of your deranged imagination."

His hands were at my throat.

I shoved him, for a second time that day.

He fell backwards over the railing of the belvedere with nothing but air to sustain him.

I listened: for the sliding gravel of the precipice, for the thud of a body landing on the rocks below, for a splash in case he had managed to clear the steep incline. For a long time I listened but heard nothing except Wells' scream, which persists even now.

I do not know whether Wells drowned or broke his neck or vanished into thin air like his Time Traveler. I did not search in the morning for his body. (Yes, the sun did rise, although there have been times when it didn't; but this truth I wouldn't dare admit to Mrs. Willoughby!) Of course, Wells lived on *somewhere* and finished *somewhere* his *Outline of History*; saw it published—*somewhere*; relished his acclaim—*somewhere*; continued to enjoy his power over women. But he also died as a result of his fall from Mrs. Willoughby's belvedere. For so I imagine it. And so, therefore, it is.

(Am I insane?

I wonder.

And don't care.

Knowing that Africa will love me—sane or not.)

I was asleep and dreaming of Mrs. Willoughby. Her piano-colored hair—how rich and fragrant. Her breasts—so full and milky. Her nails—sharp and red. And her hat was charming, too, though I do not as a rule notice millinery.

I stroked her thigh—her "silken" thigh. Why not? One cannot always be minting new metaphors! I stroked her thigh and nibbled happily at this and that, exulting in her return from Kong's jungle fastness.

The Bishop dragged himself out from under the bed, his crosier clattering.

"Adulterer! Fornicator!" he thundered. "And now you've committed murder because of your unholy lust!"

Mrs. Willoughby hid her face and wept for Wells, whose prowess would not now be tested on Prince Albert Street.

I knocked the Bishop down. In return he smote me with his crosier.

"Beast!" he fulminated. "Sodomite!"

In a fine rage I set upon him, strangling him with his cassock rope. He made a nasty adenoidal sound before crumpling like a paper bag onto the floor.

"Is he dead?" Mrs. Willoughby asked, amid sobs.

"Yes," I said, well satisfied.

I lugged the body out of doors and left it for the wild animals, which entered the city after dark.

"You are cruel," said Mrs. Willoughby when I returned. She was brushing her nervous hair, which crackled. "It will thunder tonight," she said.

"Would you like to go to the theater?"

"What's on?" she asked, watching me closely in the cheval glass.

"*Macbeth*."

I bit her shoulder.

"You are cruel," she repeated.

We sat in Mrs. Willoughby's box and waited for the house lights to go out so that we could fondle one another secretly. She seemed to have forgotten all about Wells. Mrs. Willoughby was never one to brood, I thought approvingly. After Lenin's deportation for "outrages

against the Bishop's Turkish carpet," she had scarcely turned a hair
before taking up with von Höhnel, the polo champion.

"Are we dreaming?" she asked while the Three Witches cackled.

"Yes."

And as proof, I levitated.

"Good," she said.

We watched the play, taking comfort in the dark. And in each
other's hands, which behaved like little animals.

Banquo's ghost appeared during Macbeth's reception. I was
wondering how people managed in those days without cocktails when
the Bishop leapt from the wings.

"Murderer!" he screamed at me, shaking his crosier.

Never shake thy gory locks at me!

"I thought he was dead," said Mrs. Willoughby.

"He is. This is the Bishop's ghost."

"Are you sure we're asleep?" she asked anxiously.

I shrugged. One is never entirely sure of anything in Africa.

I wrote a little in my *History of the Imagination*, like Samuel
Pepys writing in his diary centuries before. Like his, mine is in ci-
pher: those who read it will not understand its true meaning.

If, in fact, I do.

Mrs. Willoughby was asleep under the mosquito net, her beautiful body naked in the agitated light that beat up and down the glass
chimney on the writing desk. She is enfolded in history, I thought.
The big history, the public one, and mine—the marvelous history.
Wells called it a lie, but I do not believe that. What can be imagined,
is. This I believe. The movements of the brain, the heart—the landscape of the body and desire—these are worth setting down. History is a story, I told Wells, who had come to sit on the side of the
bed to watch Mrs. Willoughby sleep. One of many. Moriarty, Holmes,

Arthur Conan Doyle. The Time Traveler, the Invisible Man, H. G. Wells. All equally real and unreal.

"We're all creations," I asserted. "The products of desire. And imagination is a precondition of desire."

"I've come to take her away," he said, as if in answer.

You're not the first. I was thinking of Kong. But she returns, always, because the strength of my imagination is greater even than that of desire.

Wells lifted the netting.

"And the war that's coming…will your imagination be proof against that?" he asked, reading my mind.

His anguished look pained me, moved me to unwonted sympathy.

"Leave us," I said gently; and, being but a figment, he left, having no choice but to do as I wished.

I blew out the lamp, undressed, and lay down beside Mrs. Willoughby. She did not stir and I had no wish to wake her. The day had been long. I had murdered and created. Tomorrow would come (with or without the sun's rising), and we would pick up the thread again.

Outside, the Bishop's ghost stole past the French windows, dragging its crosier soundlessly.

And the war that's coming? I asked of the engulfing darkness.

I listened a moment, but no answer came to me from out of the night.

Only thunder over Kilindini Harbor.

EXTREME CRUELTY

With the murder of the Bishop, I entered my final and most heroic phase of cruelty. I plumed myself in the brilliant feathers of spite, robed myself in a magisterial iconoclasm. I beheaded the public monuments and ravaged the Governor's flowerbeds. I stormed the citadels of virtue and muddied the waters of morality. I stooped by the ditch in which the murdered wayfarers had been thrown and withheld my tears. My perversions were various, their satisfaction immediate and inventive. In short, I became the most anathematized man in Africa.

The Bishop's successor inveighed against me, calling on God to smite me in my body's sensitive places.

The governments of Africa issued dire warnings against those who would give me succor.

The constabulary featured me on handbills, promising inflationary rewards for my capture.

The Nairobi Opera Company, whose performance I had mocked and shambled, gave benefit concerts for those pledged to my destruction.

My mother was persuaded to denounce me to the newspapers on five continents. And Anna—Anna, whom I loved with the cruelty of a hopeless passion—refused to visit me in my dreams.

"You should ask their forgiveness," said the jackal, whose mouth was occupied with dripping wildebeest haunch. "Humble yourself, seek absolution, expiate your crimes by good works, and pray for mercy."

I was incredulous!

"The life of a haunted animal is no life at all," the jackal continued. "Believe me, I know what I'm talking about: I was with Rimbaud in Harar."

I doubted jackals have so long a life expectancy but decided against a challenge, knowing well their savagery when crossed.

"Rimbaud lived in a state of nature," I said instead. "His life, like his poetry, was cruel."

"You are not of the same stuff!" he sneered.

Offended, I rose up and killed the jackal. I trampled his body underfoot and flung it into the ravine.

"Rimbaud's cruelty is nothing next to mine!" I gloated, as I walked towards the horizon that was writhing in the terrible heat at midday.

Shortly after 3:00, I entered the alabaster city and stood among its trembling houses.

A missionary leaped out of a church door and thrust a devotional tract into my hands.

"Profit by the Word or reap the Whirlwind!" she brayed.

I folded her into a pamphlet in which I wrote a polemic of my own in favor of Cruelty.

A soldier flew at me, lance glinting in a sun whose only purpose is to engender maggots.

"Hooligan!" he shouted, hoarse with indignation.

Laughing, I wrapped a python round his ankles so that he fell on his lance. And then, for good measure, I twisted it.

"Oh, you are a cruel bastard!" he said with his dying breath.

An avenging angel swooped down from the roof. Gathering his iron skirts, he clattered towards me, his ancient face rouged with rust.

I disliked him immediately and toppled him with sharp words.

To punish my impieties, God caused Himself to be lowered from the empyrean by an ingenious system of ropes and pulleys.

"I don't give *that*"—I snapped my fingers theatrically—"for such a clumsy and old-hat *deus ex machina*!"

Nature shuddered, but what was Nature to me? I rolled up my sleeves and prepared to do violence to the Almighty, Ancient of Days.

I shredded Him.

And He repaired Himself.

I crumbled Him.

And He restored Himself.

I dispersed Him.

And He reconstituted Himself.

I blew Him to bits with everlasting sticks of dynamite.

And He reassembled Himself.

I sundered Him, and He rejoined Himself. I interrupted Him, and He resumed Himself. I adjourned Him, and He reconvened Himself. I perforated Him, and He performed holy acts of closure. I peeled Him, but He only laughed—the old fox!—and could not be tricked into repealing Himself in order to end up sitting among the superannuated gods.

And now God went on the offensive.

He beat me with trees and stony crags of mountains. With millstones and fluted columns did He beat me, and also with small Rhenish castles. (He drubbed me and dashed me—don't for a moment imagine otherwise! And He dunked me in oceans as well!) Afterwards we grappled, and there was an uncomfortable entanglement of molecules—ignoble and divine—that was disentangled only with great difficulty.

I was, however, unimpressed: He hardly made a dent in me.

"Ha!" I scoffed.

And though He opened the ground and showed me the running fire, the fuse, and the unraveling cable that binds together all things— I scorned Him.

Disheartened, He climbed back into the machine and made His slow and creaking ascent—an old man, never to set foot on earth again.

Nature groaned and shook dust into the air, covering the sun.

I traveled on, to a country untenanted by man, and stood before a mirror in an otherwise empty room.

"Mirror, mirror, on the wall—who's the cruelest of them all?" I asked.

"You," said the mirror.

And so, having become the epitome of cruelty, I renounced it at last, and took up goodness with all the relentlessness that is in my nature.

But oh, what a fine wallow I had in the days of extreme cruelty!

THE CATALOGUE

Dr. Landis threw up his hands and wept. He did so in the honorable way of a man who has come to the end of his strength. Africa had frustrated his attempts to classify its parts. We did not fault him, but his despair sent a shiver through us. He had arrived from the Smithsonian with sufficient enthusiasm, tags, and string to label everything—or so he thought. But the final days of our journey as we approached the limits of our experience had confounded his and all science. He was not the first to delude himself that Africa is manageable. One by one we had failed and accepted our failure.

We picked him up where he lay gnashing his teeth in the dust and carried him into the tent. The heated canvas smelled like a musty attic. The light seeping through the tent flap looked like the yellowing pages of an old book. The insects under the floorboards creaked like a rusty gate. We took comfort in similes—by God we did! Each was a cosmology, each a map of the unknown. In our place you would feel the same—so far from home and lost to all that is familiar. But the trouble with Africa is that ultimately it destroys similes. Their referents vanish in the impenetrable underbrush. Only occasionally are we permitted ("vouchsafed," the Bishop used to say) a fleeting glimpse of them through the thorn bushes, under the leaves, trembling at the bottom of some great ravine. But a glimpse is all, and soon Africa closes its hand.

I held the *papier-mâché* curiosity that had undone Dr. Landis and came to a decision.

I sent for Dewey, whose Decimal System had organized the world of knowledge.

He did not come willingly.

My emissaries had to apply force at several strategic points. He yelped. I was remorseful. But it was necessary.

He stood in the clearing, rubbing his eyes in disbelief. His hair needed brushing. His shoes were untied and ridiculously inappropriate for the wilderness. He had not had time to put on a collar. His fingers were covered with tiny decimals and letters of the alphabet. I gave him my tent, my delicate blue willow washbowl. He washed his inky fingers. I lent him a brush, a collar, some sensible shoes, and a broad-brimmed hat to keep off the sun.

He was mollified, but only just.

"Why have you brought me here?" he demanded in a dry voice that threatened to crack.

"We need help with the cataloguing," I said. "Our explorations have come to a standstill because of this"—I showed him the curiosity—"and other unclassifiable phenomena. What is needed, Melvil—may I call you Melvil?"

He indicated that I mightn't.

"What is urgently required, Mr. Dewey, is a system!"

My colleagues applauded. All two hundred porters dropped their burdens and began a week-long celebration in my honor. I blushed with pleasure.

"But this is not a library!" shouted Dewey.

"There are more things in heaven and earth than are dreamt of in your library," I retorted to great effect, I thought.

My colleagues agreed. I was the man of the hour.

Seeing our resolve, Dewey rolled up his sleeves and set to work.

Dewey supervised the building of the cabinet to house the card catalogue. He took as his model the Ark of the Covenant as described in the Book of Exodus:

> And they shall make an ark of shittim wood:
> two cubits and a half shall be the length thereof,
> and a cubit and a half the breadth thereof,
> and a cubit and a half the height thereof.

We built it to withstand the sun and rain and worms. With brass and irony did we fit it and on rubber tires mount it. One month did we labor, such was the hardness of the wood, the obduracy of the metals, the intractability of the porters. In the end we had a cabinet of substance. Its forthright affirmation of three and only three dimensions comforted us.

Dewey was satisfied.

"You may call me Melvil," he said.

To begin with, we catalogued the exotic—"in alphabetical order":

the black bulbul, the Boer, the dik-dik, the frankolin, the kangaroo rat, the kob, the mongoose, the monitor lizard, the nightjar, the paradise flycatcher, the pocket gopher, the purple ibis, the red bulbul, the yellow bat.

Next the esoteric: *epimys nieventrisulae, graphiurus parvus, lophurmys aquilus, oenomys hypoxanthus bacchante, otomys irroratus tropicalis, paraxerus jacksoni, pedetes surdaster, tatera varia Heller, thamnomys surdaster polionops, zelotomys hildegardae.*

Then the erotic, for the Library of Congress—the details of which I am forbidden to publish—and finally, after a lengthy passage, several strange alphabets that I have not the keys to reproduce here.

The landscape became difficult; our advance slowed. We towed the cabinet tirelessly behind us, bogging down all too often in obscure matter. Dewey lashed our already striped backs. We lost the trail and entered a *papier-mâché* mush. We argued among ourselves whether this was not the primordial matter with which an illusory nature constituted itself as reality.

Dewey scoffed.

"Nature is bedrock," he asserted. "Reality sits upon it. Illusion is the theater of con artists, magicians, and priests. All things are classifiable. What isn't doesn't count."

He returned to his ceaseless cataloguing. The file drawers opened to receive each new card, written in his neat hand. Our taxonomy was stretched to the breaking point.

"Pop!" it went finally with a popping that could be heard for miles around. The center, which we had occupied, which had moved with us every step of the way, moved elsewhere. Saturated, we entered the realm of the purely subjective. Our ears rang.

We found existence on the periphery disturbing. We plotted our position on the X-Y grid, but it kept slipping.

"Slippage!" shouted Quigley. "God have mercy on us all!"

No longer at the center of things, how could we possibly separate one object from another so as first to identify, then classify it? This was the nub of our terror.

Dewey remained calm. He stood on the top of the cabinet for all to see. He was a striking figure in the dying light.

"Courage, men!" he counseled. "The catalogue is nearly complete. There remains but one drawer to fill."

Our spirits lifted.

"Hooray!" we shouted.

"But first, rest a while," he said kindly, so that we loved him.

We rested. The world came flooding back. Things returned to normal; that is, our former relationship to them was restored.

"Onward!" exhorted Dewey.

"Onward!" we answered.

At last we came to the end of things. Dewey was not surprised.

"It was to be expected," he said. "In a finite space there can be only a finite number of things. Or, if you prefer, when God rested on the seventh day, creation came to an end."

We nodded in agreement.

Shortly after, we encountered the Very Last Thing. Because we had been inching our way back in time with every step forward, it also happened to be the First Thing. (Surely you can see that!) Dewey took off his hat and slowly approached it.

"Behold!" he exclaimed. "A & Ω. The Irreducible Object!"

He lifted it carefully for all to see.

We made suitable sounds of awe.

(What was it like, you ask?

It was like nothing. It was like everything. It confounded simile. It was incomparable!

Was it beautiful?

Who can say?

Was it worth the journey?

Impossible to tell.)

With the Great Work finished, Dewey returned to America and his library. Whether he was ever the same again, I do not know. How the journey may have changed me, I didn't have time to consider. The catalogue had to be brought out. We were tired of reading Africa in the original! We needed to disengage ourselves a while from the extremes of experience. We needed therapy followed by a period of convalescence.

We would sit in our tents and study the cards. Little by little, Africa would fade and with it our terror.

NERVOUSNESS

I had omitted Tangier. It is a serious and unthinkable and even grievous omission, they said, one after another, coming to my tent at sunset and later when the moon rose, beaten into a bronze parenthesis. Its light sat warily in my spoon.

"You must add Tangier to the itinerary at once!" they threatened with raised voices, such was their need. And mine, too, because of the killing we had done and the years of deprivation. They shook their fists at me—the best of men—each a Kipling. Each possessing courage and a stout heart.

I was powerless to resist them because of their goodness and because I was having a nervous breakdown. Africa had made me porous. Its limitless gardens, its perfumes, its plagues—they penetrated me. In the absence of women, I had forgotten myself. In the absence of a dainty foot, I had grown solemn and coarse. Imagine the human heart, its plush appointments and dazzling valves become wooden—a box to keep potatoes in. Or munitions catalogues.

No, we must have Tangier though the undertaking come to grief! Tangier and its evocations of fruit and bird, beaded curtains undulating in the Arab quarter, sweating sherbet cups, and jeweled navels.

I called Ali and Shemlani, my faithful tent boys. I ordered them to strike the tents. I ran outside and shouted into the velvet ear of night: "Strike the tents, men! We leave at once for Tangier!"

Stravinsky polished his wire-rims on the tablecloth. He was nervous. The strain, he said, it's too much for me. He looked bad. I took his temperature with my safari thermometer, counting *one, two, three, four....* He sat across the table, perspiration beading in his thin hair.

"You have a fever," I said, shaking down the thermometer. I wiped it clean with Bombay Gin and returned it to my medical kit.

"Things are falling apart," he said, putting his glasses back on.

He had fled Paris after the *succès de scandale* of his *Rite of Spring.* Grocers rioting at the Ballets Russes! he said irritably. Bank clerks complaining of shifting time signatures.

"Swine! They came only to see Tamara's legs!"

"You are too violent," I told him. "The world wants pretty things. Go back to Diaghilev, beg his forgiveness, and write another *Petrushka.* Or *Firebird.*"

"Ah!" he said. "*The Firebird.* The most striking of all the tanagers is called the firebird. I think that is why I came to Tangier—because of the mental association."

"We live our lives by accident," I said, stirring my couscous.

"Not our art!" he answered hotly.

That, too, will come, but I did not tell him so. He was on the edge, and I had no wish to nudge him over.

A silence ensued during which fat flies banged against the screen, the sticky blades of the fan turned in the heavy air, and, outside, beyond the road and stretch of beach, the Mediterranean swayed.

"War will be the death of many things," he said at last. "Fabergé eggs, the fluted columns of the classical age, ragtime."

He sighed profoundly and went to bed. A good man, out of place in the world's rough and tumble.

I went out into the street. The sudden sun stung my eyes. A black curtain dropped. I raised it and walked to the harbor to listen a while to the creaking machine.

"Igor," I prayed. "Thrive in your art. We have need of you. But beware the swamp of eccentricity. The noise of universal derailment is not music to our ears though it may be to yours."

I emptied my pockets into the harbor.

Red and white boats. The water blue, dashed with pink sunlight.

The world likes pretty things.

I turned my mind to women.

The women were arranged on pillows. They were pink; the pillows, damask. The women were comely. I drank absinthe and demitasse. The women parted their caftans with their knees. I smoked a Turkish cigarette. The women laughed arabesques. I looked through the lozenge-shaped windowpanes at ruby and green clouds. The women showed me a straw-colored monkey, an emerald cuckoo, a book of illustrations needing no explanation. I fingered tortoise combs with strands of copper and gold hair caught in the clips. The women lit incense and played a thin, shrill music on the gramophone in which I became lost. I followed the soft padding of bare feet on the marble, on the parquet, on the carpet. I watched the women undress the bed of its silk sheet. I watched the women undress.

I could have stayed with them forever, caught in a shaft of sunlight, splashed with moonlight, veiled in silk and smoke. I could have stayed happily outside nature and necessity. But the old nervousness returned, doubtless aggravated by absinthe and tobacco. A curious sexual vagueness followed. My head droned with "Christiné's Song" as I had heard Dranem sing it in 1905:

> We were driving through fields of lotuses;
> I left my navel there, you left your umbrella,
> I lost my number there, you lost your humerus.
> I was your pink pebble and you were my quail.

I strangled the pillows in an access of impotent rage. I shredded the sheet and plucked the cuckoo. The women ran into the street in their caftans. They watched through the ruby and green windowpanes as I caught the monkey by its tail.

There followed a stay behind white walls, savoring the wisteria, drinking aromatic teas, eating yogurt, fruit, parts of sheep. I enjoyed hydraulic treatments and wholesome stimulations. Quigley paid solicitous visits on Thursday afternoons. Carlson and Lane were denied entrance because of their outrageous behavior towards the nuns.

Recovered, I was returned to history and my self.

War. Mustard gas and the muddy trench. Ash.
Armistice.

Then jazz, bobbed hair, and the brothels nationalized. The world grew unrecognizable.

Stravinsky in Switzerland not answering my telegrams.

The Gaîté-Rochechouart closed.

Ffft! Ffft! Ffft!

Stravinsky in Paris not returning my telephone calls.

My nervousness before women. My nervousness before art. My nervousness before Bolshevism. My nervousness before recently discovered particles. My nervousness before the ever-expanding table of elements. My nervousness before the pronouncements of Freud. My nervousness before Relativity. My nervousness before the sun, which is apparently cooling.

It was then I asked myself the overwhelming question: How am I to live in the present age?

I could not answer.

And knowing there was no place else on earth I understood as well, I returned to Africa. To its heart. Where all questions become meaningless.

THE GEOLOGY OF LOVE

He had been dead many years when he finally arrived in Africa. Long enough to devolve into an egg custard, he said. A *blancmange*. Though meant in jest, I thought his remark tasteless and told him so. *Humph*! he peeved, tugging at his beard.

"I ought to have no earthly existence at all," Darwin continued in that smug way of his. "After all I've been through."

"My friend Pennington is also dead," I told him, hoping to puncture the inflated opinion he had of himself.

"Yes, I met the gentleman."

"Where?" I asked suspiciously.

(You recall I returned Pennington to the wild forest people in the condition I had found him: rather worse for wear—he was a corpse after all!—and, if not talkative, glumly capable of speech if incapable of satisfying my curiosity concerning the hereafter.)

"Where did you meet him?" I repeated, nudging him with the toe of my boot from his rapt contemplation of the dirt.

"In the Sweet-by-and-by," said Darwin—maliciously, for I knew him to be an unrepentant materialist, who had given his name to a pernicious and irreligious science. "Outside time, where all times are one and the equality of death places everyone on an equal footing."

"Pennington would have nothing to do with you," I sneered. "He is a lady's man."

"Shit!" said Darwin, and snuffled disagreeably.

"Pardon me?" I asked, ready to take offense.

"I have mistaken this dried rhino dung for a bit of Paleozoic stratum." He snuffled a second time. "My nose is not what it used to be."

"Did you see Pennington in the forest?" I demanded.

"Here and there," said Darwin. "Here, there, and everywhere!"

And he brayed a laugh that set my hairs on end!

"I should like to kill you," I told him in all sincerity, "if it were only still possible."

"All things are possible…" he said. "But not that!" he hastened to add.

I sighed and, hearing the silver bell announce the cocktail hour, turned on my heel and left him to his dung.

"I met the most annoying man."

"Oh?" Colette said, allowing a long blue plume of cigarette smoke to leak from her mouth.

My eyes watered the way they always did in the presence of strong tobacco. (Siggy's cigars are the worst, and I insisted that my analysis be conducted in *plein-air*.)

"Charles Darwin," I said.

"I thought he was dead."

"His ideas persist and, with them, the man."

The elegant sophism pleased me immensely, and I looked to her for admiration. She withheld it, absorbed as she was in the ember at the end of her Abdulla.

I sat at the bar and developed my idea: those who leave us, finally, with a body of work seem to be with us always, seem as if they not only breathed air yet, but breathed the same air as we. But what of those who leave nothing behind? Are we to be cheated of eternity simply because our brains are not so evolved?

I was angry. I picked up my double-barreled Holland and let fly at the King, his portrait which hung over the bar.

Colette jumped inside her dress.

The barman picked up a decorative Masai spear and flung it at me, "for indignities against His Majesty."

Pritchett, chief of the Mombasa constabulary, materialized with a squad of handsome askari policemen, all creased khakis and polished shoes.

"It was only an effigy!" I insisted, referring to the King's blasted portrait.

I was standing before the judge, trying to suppress the urge to laugh at his judicial wig, which, for some reason, was in motion atop his head like a hedgehog.

"It was only an effigy," I repeated.

"Silence!" screamed the judge, who was in no mood for subtleties. "I have had you before me on two previous occasions: once for creating a public disturbance by parading the corpse of your friend Pennington—"

"A fetish!" I interrupted.

Again, the judge adjured me to silence.

"And a second time for the murder of the Bishop of Mombasa."

The Bishop stood and showed himself, the marks the cassock rope had left on his neck still visible.

"Not proved!" my lawyer objected.

"He is the man!" the Bishop screeched, shaking an accusatory finger at me. "He is my murderer!"

The Bishop's words created an immediate sensation in the courtroom.

"Inadmissible!" my lawyer shouted above the din. "The words of a ghost have no weight in jurisprudence." (I watched the Bishop's words rise through the ceiling, each a gaudy-colored balloon reminding me of lingerie.) A patron of the Mombasa Theatrical Society, my lawyer quoted Hamlet:

> The spirit that I have seen
> May be the devil, and the devil hath power
> T' assume a pleasing shape....

Considering that the Bishop's shape—quick or dead—was far from pleasing, I let my eyes rove until they came to rest, happily, on someone whose was.

Colette.

Will I become her lover? I wondered.

"I could have sent you to the gallows," said Darwin, with characteristic smugness. "I was a witness to the Bishop's murder—deserve it though he might. The view from the next evolutionary rung is excellent."

"The testimony of an atheist would not be believed."

"But I'm buried in Westminster Abbey!" he protested.

"And I wish you would return there at once. I don't mean to be unkind," I said, relenting. "But I've had a bellyful of great men! Africa is a Mecca for them! And it has been my fate to meet them—one and all." I sighed. "You can have no idea how wearisome that is: to be subjected, morning, noon, and night, to the genius of others."

I regarded my gin—the little glass of it that sat peremptorily before me on the bar of the Mombasa Hotel.

Darwin blew his nose into an enormous handkerchief.

"What do you want?" I asked him. "What is it that you want in Africa?"

"To find the missing link! Evidence of the species that once stood between man and ape. Mediator between the human and the simian world."

"Oh, you mean Kong," I replied.

"In your arms life reasserts itself," I told Colette as we snuggled under the mosquito net. We were in my room, not far from Freud's office on Queen Victoria Street. I took courage in his nearness. "Desire beats up inside me, and death retreats."

I was sincere. I did feel the icy grip of death let go as Colette rummaged me. Death let go its hand and retreated, although only a little way. I saw it standing in the corner of the room where the shadows were thickest.

"My *chéri*," she breathed into my ear, moistening it with her tender words.

My fingertips read the formations of hips, buttocks, and bone, the pelvic estuary, the mounds of her breasts. In return her hands traced butte and plain; her lips, brushing mine, banished doubt; and with her hair she swept away a bitter unhappiness.

"It is the geology of love," said Darwin, for whom there could be no secrets.

Colette was asleep, and he had stepped out of the closet to speak to me.

"The lover digs and, digging, discovers his lost self in the beloved. Digs with a spade soft as feathers, down through the sediment of time and habit until the shining ore of youth is uncovered. To be gloried in."

The sight of our lovemaking had temporarily aroused his long insensate body and with it a Swinburnian rapture.

"I wish I were a boy again, in Shrewsbury, undressing a girl for the first time behind the hayricks." He lifted the mosquito net and looked at Colette. "She's beautiful," he said, and in his voice I heard the tremolo of desire. And then he sighed for, being one of the dead, he knew the fate of every living thing on earth.

"Geological forces are marking her, eroding her. This lovely flesh will press against the sheets of time and leave its fossil record there. An invalid in the Palais-Royal Hotel, she will climb into her last bed, in Paris, on August 3, 1954. Soon, no one will be living who remembers her face or these sweet hills." He reached out a hand to touch her breast, hesitated, and in that hesitation I saw the struggle of non-being to enter the mortal world. He withdrew his hand, sadly.

"Alas!" he said, for he was a Victorian after all and entitled to his anachronisms.

"Prince Kong is in town," I said, closing the mosquito net over Colette's nakedness. "I suspect he's come for her."

Darwin was incensed.

"I'll castrate the rapscallion!" he shouted. "I'll display his pickled member to the great British public! The indignities suffered by the Elephant Man will be as nothing next to his!"

I led him outside onto the balcony to calm him with a view of the busy street. But he would not be calmed.

Darwin was in love.

"You've made a new conquest," I told Colette as we were eating our breakfast in the Mombasa Hotel Grille.

"Oh?" she asked, buttering her toast.

"Charles Darwin."

"Such a dreary man."

"Where is your novelist's curiosity?" I taunted her.

"Nothing could induce me to satisfy it with him!"

And in the crunching of a piece of toast, I heard the bones of past lovers.

Just then, Kong appeared, dressed as he had been for the abduction of Mrs. Willoughby: tuxedo, top hat, spats, and yellow gloves—the very image of an effete dandy. If I didn't know him to be dangerous, I would have laughed. He bowed mockingly at me and then, setting eyes on Colette, swaggered over to our table.

"I gave you back your Mrs. Willoughby," he smirked. "She no longer interests me. But this—" He took Colette's hand and kissed it. "This lovely lady is of supreme interest."

Colette yawned and took her hand away.

Kong's lips retreated in a sneer, uncovering his formidable teeth.

"We shall see," he said imperiously, pulling off his gloves.

"There *is* someone who would like to know you better," I said with happy spite.

"And who might that be?"

"Charles Darwin."

"That ass!" he snarled. "Absurd to think I could have anything in common with you or your cretinous kind!" He stood and beat his breast. "I am the culmination, the flowering and highest expression of my species—a species infinitely superior to you poor, bald, sexually repressed humans!"

In his indignation he would have leapt onto the chandelier if I had not restrained him.

"We are absolutely not related!" he shouted.

Evidently, evolution was a sore point with him, too.

Colette was amused.

"So mankind did not descend from the monkeys?" she asked.

Kong composed himself and, after a moment, replied haughtily, "Insofar as man is a degenerate of my race—yes, he can be said to have descended. Apes are perfect in the way anything is perfect that is *completed*. As you still struggle to be."

He pulled on his gloves and, turning to Colette, icily concluded, "If men and monkeys are related, it is—I assure you—only distantly and not a family connection we are pleased to acknowledge."

"He's a very virile man," said Colette admiringly.

"He's not a man. He's a beast!"

I was annoyed. Kong had ruined one love affair, and I was determined not to let him spoil my chances with Colette.

"All men are beasts," she replied.

Knowing full well the truth of this, I was momentarily silenced. I took advantage of the silence to caress her. If all men are beasts, I might as well behave beastly.

"Not now, I'm writing!" she scolded.

"Why don't you use a typewriter?"

"The machine isn't sensuous."

I returned to my caresses.

"Nothing is more sensuous than a devoted lover," I whispered.

She shook her head.

"Words," she said. "Words are the most sensuous thing of all."

(How I hate writers and their paradoxes!)

I lay on the bed and sulked while her pen *scratched, scratched, scratched* through the hot afternoon.

"Kong has debauched Mrs. Willoughby," I said.

Colette smiled.

I closed my eyes and slept.

And woke to find her gone.

"I envy him," I said.

"It is always so," Darwin replied wistfully. "The more evolved species yearns nostalgically for its primitive ancestor. The fish dreams of plankton, indolent in sunlight. The salamander, of a worm eating its way through the chocolate earth. Modern men long to exchange their politics and poetry, their brass bands and flying-machines for the frank and sauntering ways of animals."

And as if he had sailed all the way from St. Louis in order to illustrate this very point, Cromwell Dixon passed overhead in his cigar-shaped blimp.

"What wouldn't he give to be a bird!" said Darwin. "Even an *archaeopteryx* winging through empty Jurassic skies."

Cromwell waved to us, and we returned his greeting, wishing him well though he looked awkward and ridiculous above the streets of Mombasa. A foolish, flimsy poem of flight.

"What do you long for?" I asked Darwin, as an unaccustomed tenderness rose up in me.

"The creature from which *I* have descended," he answered. "A boy in Shrewsbury. A young man in Tierra del Fuego and Port Desire. An old man retired happily in Kent. I envy the living."

I met Colette at the bar. She had been with Darwin. She had been curious, after all, to know him better.

"From the point of view of the novelist," she said; but I suspected her curiosity was that of a woman for a man—a genius, after all, of immense experience and renown.

He had, she said, disappointed.

He had, she said, no romance.

They had stood looking out to sea. The water hissed and sighed. The moon was copper; the black sky, dusted with stars.

She invited him to look at the moon, but he looked at shells instead—"the ocean's broken crockery."

The stars! she pleaded, but he was transfixed by what lay under his feet.

"I am no romantic," he said.

"But doesn't the lovely Mombasa night move you?" she demanded.

"I can no longer be moved," he replied.

"Sadly," she told me. "So that I pitied him."

She had taken his hand. He permitted it.

"His hand was cold," she told me.

"What did you expect?" I asked angrily.

"Why are you angry?"

I shrugged. I didn't know.

She took my hand. She wanted to feel its warmth. She was suddenly afraid. The shadows in the corners of the room were uncommonly dark. Night pressed against the window as if wanting to get in. At the far end of the bar, someone began to cry. I gulped down my gin. And another, "for courage." And then, holding each other's hands, we hurried upstairs to my room to forget.

A HISTORY OF THE IMAGINATION

I was sailing to Cincinnati with the King of Belgium in his private steamship. (It is not an easy thing to sail to Cincinnati from Africa! you say, cynical as always. Though a river town, Cincinnati is far from the world's great oceans! Except in dreams, I say—in dreams Cincinnati is an easy sail from Africa, especially in a ship such as belongs to the King of All the Belgians with its wonderful featherbeds, its frequent cocktail hours announced by the ship's silver bell, its golden ropes and handsome sailors who speak, I suppose, Walloon.) I was accompanying the King to the funeral for the last passenger pigeon, which had died the day before in the

Cincinnati Zoo. (You cannot travel from the Congo to Cincinnati in only a day! you shout, fit to be tied. Tut-tut! I say, not at all troubled by such questions of travel. For me, travel had become a thought.)

"We have a special fondness for pigeons," the King said as we stood at the rail and watched the whales rush through the ocean like locomotives. "Pigeon racing is the national sport of Belgium, you know."

I did not know.

"My people are in mourning for this bird."

He showed me a photograph of the people of Belgium—not all of them, of course, but as many as can be crowded into a downtown street. They were dressed in black from head to toe. Black crepe drooped from lampposts and in shop windows and even from the sky, although that might have been a smudge or a photographer's trick.

"It is sad," the King said, hanging his head.

"Yes."

In truth I did not care that the last passenger pigeon was dead. In Africa I had eagerly helped to finish off several species of fauna. But I was anxious to see Cincinnati once more and was—let me confess it—homesick for America. With the exception of that brief time spent working in the Wright brothers' bicycle shop in Dayton (but that, too, I am now convinced, was a dream), I had not been home in eight years.

(Strange that in both cases I should have gone to Ohio! Is Ohio significant in a way that never occurred to me—that has, perhaps, never occurred to anyone?)

"It is sad," the King sighed.

The whales dove to the bottom of the ocean, to the ocean bed. Who knows if they rest or must keep moving like the shark.

We went below and ate Belgian waffles with strawberries and confectioner's sugar and talked about our safari days, and for a little while we were happy to be taking this ocean voyage.

Was the naval attaché on board, whom I'd met briefly years before in the jungles of the Belgian Congo? Certainly! There on the high seas he was in his element. He was both captain and navigator of the King's steamship. He also handed out the mops when the salt-stained decks needed swabbing and inspected them afterwards. He kept the ship's keys in his pocket, including the shiny one to the rum closet; and when the decks were swabbed to his satisfaction, he would open the closet and, as the men took off their hats and cheered, take out the bottle for swigging. Three times would the ship's swigging bottle make its circuit of the assembled sailors. At the completion of the third and final circuit, the mate would cork the bottle and hand it shyly to the naval attaché, who would lock it up again in the rum closet under his sole command. (Not even the King had the key to it.)

"That is called 'ship's discipline,'" said the naval attaché to me after I had witnessed such a swabbing and swigging. "Ours is a lovely crew," he said patriotically.

A dream crew, I thought to myself.

"Yes," he said, for the naval attaché had learned to read minds at the Institute for Psychical Research.

We traveled at the speed of thought. How could we not with so urgent an appointment to keep?

The engines? you ask.

Enormous turbines constructed of some precious metal taken from the King's mines in Africa.

Their design? you ask.

A secret.

How did the ship's hull stand the strain? you ask.

It is only imperfectly understood. But the hull was painted blue.

Did the wind fly in your face while you stood on deck? you ask.

There was no wind.

Was the noise terrible? you ask.

There was no noise. Or only a slight hum.

The King and I were taking a postprandial stroll around the deck.

The naval attaché was sighting the sun with his sextant.

The sailors were swabbing the deck or coiling the golden ropes or uncoiling them. (Their actions were often mysterious to me.)

It began to rain ("because of nature's sorrow," said the King). The naval attaché hurried indoors, afraid to get his sextant wet.

I seemed to see two Kikuyu men. They clasped each other in a tight embrace as they walked through the waves under a battered old umbrella.

"Do you see that?" I asked the King, pointing at an area of gray ocean.

He shook his head.

"You may call me Leo," he said. "Because of all we have been through together."

The naval attaché knocked at my cabin door.

"Come in," I called.

He did and stood in the doorway with his boat-shaped hat in his hands.

"We have reached Cincinnati," he said.

My face partially lathered, I looked through the porthole at the city of my youth and was disappointed that it did not shine as it had always done in memory.

"It is the fault of the rain," he said, having looked into my mind and seen the disappointment there.

"You are very sympathetic for a naval attaché," I told him.

He bowed and left me to finish my shaving.

Cincinnati! How wonderful your streets and houses! Even in the rain. And the women on your streets and in your houses—how lovely! Why did I ever leave you for Africa? What did I hope to find in Africa that could not be found here?

And the women of Mombasa? you ask.

True, the women of Mombasa are beautiful.

And the women of Nairobi? you ask.

Also beautiful. But the women of Cincinnati were there on my doorstep. I had only to open the door and invite them inside.

"What do you think of our women, Leo?" I asked the King.

He gave me a dark look that matched the sky. If the human head were capable of launching thunderbolts like the old gods, he would have launched them at me.

He rebuked me thus: "May I remind you of the solemnity of the occasion?"

We walked to the zoo—I, a few steps behind the King, out of respect but also shame.

In the rain.

September 1, 1914. My impressions of the funeral for the last passenger pigeon: a gray and cloud-blown day. People dressed in black. The flag at half-staff. Sousa slowly marching through the zoo's black, iron gate, in a black uniform. He stands in the rain and blows a dirge on his sousaphone. On a telegraph wire overhead, three pigeons (of a species, for the time being, extant) tuck their heads under their wings and mourn. The King stands, his eyes wet. The men take off their hats. The women bow their heads. The King orates. He orates well. Soon all eyes are wet (and not with rain, you cynic!). He finishes. All is quiet except the elephants. The elephants trumpet their sorrow.

Nothing shines.

You say: It did not happen like that at all. There was no funeral—Sousa did not play. The King of Belgium certainly did not come. He had more important things to worry about: the Germans. The Germans with their pointy helmets were in Belgium ("gallant little Belgium!").

I say to you: There is another history. There is another history that exists side by side with the one you know. In it all that I have told you is true. (You have never heard of it? You are reading it here: *A History of the Imagination.*)

You say: But such a history is a figment!

I say to you: All histories lie.

You say: Then why not make the bird *live*, in its millions?

I say (without bravado but with a growing unease): I wanted to write about a funeral. I wanted to write how the King of Belgium and Sousa came to Cincinnati and stood in the rain.

You: Monster!

I: What is one bird, even the last bird of its kind, next to the millions of our kind who would shortly begin to die? I did not want to write *that* history.

Your history does them a disservice—all those people who died in the real history!

I could do nothing for them.

You shout at me: Crackpot! Nothing you say is verifiable! Nothing.

You shake your head. Maybe nothing can be proved in Africa;

but in Cincinnati, things are not so mysterious.

The funeral was over. The last passenger pigeon was buried in a shoebox under a pear tree. (*The bird was stuffed*! you scream.) Leo and I left Cincinnati.

"I will never return," I told him.

"Nor I," he said.

"I have been too long in Africa."

"And what about all the pretty women?" asked Leo.

I shrugged a helpless little shrug.

"There are other things in life besides love," I said (or perhaps it was Leo, who said it—I cannot remember).

We walked out of Cincinnati into a great forest, and in an instant the sun was shut from sight by the thick screen of wet foliage. Here and there were patches of brush, which might contain a lion, cheetah, hyena, or wild dog.

In the middle of the forest, the naval attaché was waiting to pipe us aboard.

OPENING NEW TERRITORIES

He needed writing paper. He had odd bits of paper in his coat pockets: letters from his father and Felice; a handbill advertising Madame Sosostris, "Famous Clairvoyante"; a railroad timetable picked up in Prague; a Marxist tract; a bill from a laundry on Charlotte Street, made out to the Samsas "for sheets and pillowcases." But these, he insisted, were unsatisfactory. They were soiled, their edges deckled with the hardships of travel. The folds of the letters were worn thin with repeated readings. Not that he would have used the letters. He made as if to slap my face when I suggested that he use the backs of them for his writing; the backsides were unmarked and might have served his need for paper. Evidently the idea offended him for he raised his hand and would have slapped me if I had not caught his hand in mine. I cautioned him severely. I could not allow him to strike me. Of course, I could see he was coming apart, that the jungle was too much for him. His eyes were unnaturally bright. Fever probably. Black-water fever, more than likely. He should never have come here—was a fool to come to Africa! Nevertheless, had he struck me, I would have retaliated.

"I must have writing paper!" he said, retreating into a corner of the tent. "Clean sheets—understand!—white and unsullied. *Immaculate*!" he added with unnecessary emphasis.

I confess I felt the old cruelty rise up in me as I watched his face twitch in the yellowish light from the oil lamp. I recalled with a shameful pleasure how, long ago, the nervous little Belgian had suffered at the hands of Carlson while we waited impatiently for the steamer to take us across Lake No. I was with Ross then, the one the lightning had marked. Ross, whom I have not laid eyes on since before the War. One more of the old crowd lost to me.

I poked Franz with the broom.

"Stop tormenting me!" he cried.

"Why do you need writing paper?" I said contemptuously.

"To write!" he shouted.

I poked him again.

"Behave," I admonished, "or I'll give you to the hyenas!"

"You're hurting me, sir," he said with an obsequiousness I would have considered repulsive had not his anguish peeped out from beneath it.

I put down the broom and invited him to sit.

"What do you want to write, Franz?"

"A story," he said, sitting on the trunk containing Dr. Landis' scientific paraphernalia. "About someone I knew in Prague. I woke this morning with the opening sentence in my head."

Taking a seat atop the safari liquor cabinet, I asked him to tell me it.

"*As Gregor Samsa awoke one morning from uneasy dreams,*" he recited like a schoolboy, "*he found himself transformed in his bed into a gigantic insect.*"

I got down from the liquor cabinet in order to fix myself a gin and bitters.

"In Prague, you say? I once heard of a similar case in the Congo."

He began to jump up and down in his impatience to write. I offered him a rhino steak, a tumbler of Bombay Gin, a local woman with skin the color of toffee and a tongue like velvet to distract him—but he wanted none of them.

"Only to *write*!" he said ardently.

It was then I remembered Woolworth.

F. W.—all of us called him that—had appeared as if out of no-where one afternoon at the Mombasa Hotel Bar. He looked like a man very much in need of a drink. I gave him one. A gin and tonic.

"There's quinine in the tonic water," I told him. "It's good for the malaria."

He assured me he did not have malaria.

"The day isn't over yet," I chuckled, to show him I took these things lightly—even leprosy, as I would later tell him, "which turns a man's skin to lace."

He was not amused.

He was, in fact, bemused.

"I'm not entirely sure what I'm doing here," he told us.

Quigley and Lane had joined us at the bar. They wanted to get an early start on unconsciousness. They were spending more and more time so. They wished to escape Africa as much as possible, because of their nerves. Their nerves were coming unstrung. "Like a tennis racket," said Lane, who was an avid clay-court man.

(Why did they not simply go home—to England in the case of Quigley and to America in Lane's? Have I not yet convinced you of the impossibility of leaving here! How we were transfixed by death shining everywhere around us like mica in the dirt under the equatorial sun. Even our shaving mirrors seemed to call upon us to cut our throats! Freud knew. It was in Africa that he went beyond the Pleasure Principle. I had a feeling that F. W. knew it, too.)

"Yes, you may be right," said Woolworth, who had been—I suppose—reading my mind.

I looked up from the depths of my drink into F. W.'s florid and puffy face.

"So what brings you to Africa?" I asked. "Searching for a virgin continent to deflower with your five-and-dimes?"

"I had a breakdown," he said, hanging his head in what might have been shame.

I nodded sympathetically and let him know that I, too, from time to time, have come unhinged.

"I took to my bed and wept uncontrollably," he admitted. "It's happened before—the first time after failing as a dry-goods clerk in Watertown. I went to bed then for eighteen months."

I told him how, in Africa, victims of the sleeping sickness slept for years.

"But I wasn't asleep!" he shouted.

I recharged his glass to calm him. Obviously, his nerves were still thin.

"It was too much for me," he said meekly.

"What was?"

"The Woolworth Building. What the newspaper boys call 'the Cathedral of Commerce.'" He allowed himself a flicker of a smile, which soon went out. "So many things to decide," he went on gloomily. "Granite or porphyry. Mahogany or walnut. Tile or parquet."

F. W. had personally overseen the construction of the, then, world's tallest building. It was his final bid for the admiration of Rockefeller and his gang, but they did not deign to notice the "jumped-up tradesman" with his Taft mustache.

He sighed, and in that sigh I heard the exhaustion of a once indomitable will.

I patted the back of his hand.

"Here there is nothing to decide, except whether to go on living."

The Bishop, whom I had strangled with his cassock rope, stepped out of the shadows to rebuke me: "Only the Ancient of Days can decide that!"

"Ignore him and he'll go away," I advised F. W., pointedly turning my back on the Bishop.

And in a moment, he did go, although not without upsetting our drinks with a pettish flounce of his ecclesiastical finery.

"He's as insufferable in death as he was in life," I said.

F. W. began to cry for no earthly reason.

I turned away in embarrassment.

"There is a man in Mombasa, who owns a chain of 5 & 10¢ stores," I told Franz. "Maybe he can get you some writing paper."

"Five cents, ten cents—how much is that in hellers?" he asked.

"Franz, why did you come to Africa?"

We were standing on the shore of the dismal Lorian Swamp where I had once seen Dr. Kemp eat a rhinoceros liver, which, in life, he had prized as a great delicacy.

Franz looked nervously about him at the black tree trunks, the mist, the thick leafless vines, the bubbling mud.

"I wanted a menacing *mise en scène* for a parable," he said. "One in which it is impossible to penetrate to the truth."

I nodded to show him that I understood. He was not the first writer I had met in Africa. Years before, I had fetched Arthur Conan Doyle from his encampment on the River Potha to preside over the inquest of a murdered porter.

"Africa will not disappoint you," I promised, knowing full well how unknowable everything is there.

"Cheers!"

We were happily installed in a snug corner of the Mombasa Hotel Bar, drinking champagne cocktails to each other's health. F. W. had been seeing Freud at his office on Queen Victoria Street, just around the corner from the hotel, and his analysis was going well.

"I have not cried in a week," F. W. said cheerfully.

"You look the picture of health. I wonder, do you have any paper?"

"Paper?"

F. W. reached into his pocket and took out a folded piece of paper that, when unfolded, proved to be a lithograph of Napoleon. He kissed it reverently.

"He is my hero," he said. "I have always admired his decisiveness and his conquering spirit." He searched my face as if expecting to find a mocking look there. I hid it behind my hand, anxious that he should not relapse into mawkishness. "I once had a conquering spirit, too..." he concluded, his voice trailing off into silence.

"There is a man in the jungle who needs *writing* paper," I went on. "He's very fussy about the quality. The paper must be clean and unused. He would like a watermark, although this is not essential so long as the paper is 'white and unsullied.'"

"I cannot help him," F. W. said sadly so that the heart of a more charitable man would have broken. "My inventory is all in America."

I asked him if he had transportation to America. He had none. I inquired by what power of locomotion he had arrived in Africa, but he only shrugged.

"I am not at all clear about that," he said.

I begged a ream of linen wove paper with watermark from Mrs. Willoughby. The nature of the watermark escapes me. I hurried to the Lorian Swamp with the parcel, but Franz was nowhere in sight. Dr. Kemp was there, savoring his liver. I was not surprised, knowing him to be a man of confirmed habits. Moving upwind, I asked him for information concerning Franz's whereabouts. Dr. Kemp had not fared well in death—doubtless because of his unwholesome diet— and it required a strong stomach to endure his presence. Having lost the power of intelligible speech, he could be no help to me. I made a thorough search but could find no trace of Franz. I left the parcel on the edge of the swamp in case he should return.

Years later, I read the story whose opening line he had recited in my tent. I saw nothing in it to engage either the intelligence or the sympathies. It's a monstrous travesty of nature and a waste of paper, deserving the dustbin to which I unceremoniously consigned it.

"This Gregor Samsa is no Sherlock Holmes!" I said to myself, preferring a rattling good yarn to the product of a morbid imagination.

I hurried back to Mombasa. I must say that, at the time, I did not care much for Woolworth: he was not my sort. He didn't hunt, he took no interest in the local fauna, he could not see the country- side except in a theoretical way as sites for his infernal dime stores. He did not seem to care for women and drank without enjoyment. He was not companionable, and I did not respect his fawning over the captains of industry and the wizards of finance. Still, I hurried

back to see him. Why? I don't know, unless I sensed in him someone
who could change.

When I arrived in Mombasa, he had already left for the Sahara.

2/7/15

Dear N.:

I have joined a caravan heading for the Sahara. These
Arabs interest me! They are great traders—they live, like
me, to open new territories. Sorry to run out on you like
this, but the Arabs will not wait.

Yours,
Frank Woolworth

P.S. I've paid your bar bill and instructed the barman to
keep your thirst reasonably quenched.

Sensing an adventure not to be missed, I washed the dust from my
throat, changed my socks, borrowed a horse, and headed after him.

I caught up with F. W. at El Mzereb. He looked fine in his burnoose and sat his camel well. He greeted me in Arab fashion and
invited me into his tent for goat and yogurt. As we ate, he told me
stories of his new life as an Arab trader. The Arab woman who
attended us had me "on the boil."

"You look well," I remarked.

"I am well!" he said. "These Arabs know a thing or two about
life." He pinched one of the woman's cheeks. "Yes, sir, I haven't
exhibited a hysterical symptom in weeks! And the therapy is so much
more pleasant than Dr. Freud's." Laughing good-naturedly, he
pinched the other one.

"I'm pleased to hear it," I said sincerely, wondering if I might be permitted a pinch. "When are you going back to America?"

"I'm never going back!" he shouted.

"But your five-and-dime empire..."

"I intend to open new territories beginning with a Woolworth's in El Mzereb," he announced. "I'm all through with America—and running after Rockefeller, Morgan, and those other jackals."

The Arab woman brought us sherbet.

Noting my admiration, F. W. asked, "Would you like to see her dance?"

"Very much."

He clapped his hands, and she began to dance to a shrill and intricate piping that mimicked the sound of my autonomic system. Her veils swirled in the scented breeze she herself stirred. She danced, and I trembled on the edge of dreaming. Of desiring. Of death.

I nearly fainted.

"She has that effect on some people," F. W. said with a proprietary air.

The music ceased. The figure of the dance she had woven inside the tent slowly faded. She straightened her veils and disappeared through a tent flap, letting in a dusty shaft of sunlight. I shook my head to break the spell—to shrug off my swoon.

"What will you sell in Africa?" I asked to distract myself with business.

"Pleasure," he said, lolling on a damascene pillow. "Turkish Delight," he said, unwilling to be distracted. "By the way, your friend is here."

Franz sat writing in a tent pitched at the edge of the encampment. He looked happier than I'd ever seen him. Chin propped in one hand, his pen scratched with the other a music he evidently found pleasing. I watched as he knitted a long knotted string of words. Recalling Raymond Roussel plying his "secret grammar" in a dark and stuffy cabin out in Mombasa Harbor, I wondered once more at the strange life of a writer.

"Franz, what are you doing here?"

"I'm writing a story," he said. "A parable—'Arabs and Jackals,' I call it." He put his pen down and stretched. "I met F. W.'s caravan on the way. He lent me a camel." He bounced up and down a moment on his camp stool. "It was like riding a coal bucket," he said, "through the desert night."

We left the tent and went toiling up a dune. An aeroplane flew over, dragging the dagger of its shadow across the sand. I felt the peace of the desert. In a landscape empty of any image of desire, desire left me. This is no Africa, I thought, with its endless engendering. This is bone. A jackal sidled up and licked Franz's hand. Together, we stood and watched the flaming sun drop beneath the brink of the world. The long lights changed the look of the country and gave it a beauty that had an element in it of the mysterious and the unreal.

"Tomorrow I leave for China," he said. "Although it won't be the real China anymore than this is the real Sahara. If, indeed, there *is* a real China or Sahara—or Prague, for that matter."

I felt the earth swinging through space and said nothing.

"It is all about opening new territories," he said as much to the jackal as to me. "For words. Finally, everything is words."

Suddenly sick of words, I turn away. Orion, the Bear, and the Pleiades shed what light they may while, down below, the tents shine golden on the black sand. Inside his, F. W. is dreaming, and the woman—she is dancing.

DANCING WITH THE INVISIBLE MAN

I sat in the Mombasa Hotel Bar and listened to the war.

I listened to it raging. In the gray cities across the sea. The ruined cities and blasted fields. And in the sky draggled with smoke.

From 1914 on into 1916 I listened. And shook—my hands. And drank gin and spilled it because of the shaking of my hands.

In Africa.

Freud stroked the back of my hand, telling me not to worry. The war is far away, he said. Then how is it that I hear it? I wanted to know, for I did: drifting cannonade, crack of sniper shot, the long keening of mortars, and skirl of falling bombs. And the screams,

Sigmund—the anguished screams of men! I shouted. How is it I can hear them scream?

"It is your anxiety that makes your hearing so acute," he said. "In your condition you can hear the valves of your heart open and close. Hear the fly's frenzy in the marmalade dish. The death throes of the elephants on the Kapiti Plain."

"Numb me!" I implored him.

He shook his head.

"Tranquilize me, Sigmund—put me to sleep!" I begged.

He looked at me sternly.

"You can live with anxiety," he said. "Anxiety will be the disease of the twentieth century. We will all learn to live with anxiety. But I do not wish you to become hysterical again."

He reminded me of my breakdown in Tangier and of the many months of yogurt and hydrotherapy, painful electric stimulation, the clumsy attempts to lance the abscess of desire, and of the dirty fingernails of the medical staff.

"A man like you could become lost in the winding turns of hysteria—its gray labyrinth. You might wander there forever without hope of rescue." He pierced me with his gaze and hissed, "A man of your *susceptibility*." He reminded me next of Woolworth and Caruso, both of whom had been hysterical.

In Africa.

"But Woolworth was cured!" I objected. "He went north with the Arab traders and found his grip, which was lost. And Caruso, finding his voice again, is somewhere swashbuckling with the Moroccan pirates. Hysteria is a *civilized* phenomenon."

Suddenly I understood that it was Mombasa I had to flee—Mombasa, that most European of towns. Madness is civilization; and Freud, whom I had loved these many years since my transference (one that was not yet broken), would never exorcise the demons of civilization because he was so thoroughly civilized, so...Viennese.

I stood up, resolved to turn piratical and sail in a native dhow, or buy a burnoose and join the next caravan into the desert.

"Lawrence is in Arabia," Freud said. "The war has come to the desert," he said. "Civilization has come and, with it, its discontents."

I sat. And drank my gin and let my hands shake, knowing I was helpless to stop them.

1917.

Freud believed that bodily phenomena are metaphors for the various mental disorders discovered during his research in the interior. That a twitch is an indicator of suppressed agitation. (You may recall how he dismissed Prince Kong as a mere emblem of Mrs. Willoughby's unconscious desire despite the bruises on her thigh and his big cigar, with which he overcame me as I rose in her defense.)

"It's all in your mind," Freud liked to say, belittling the importance of the body, which at that time interested me most—especially that of a woman.

"I agree with John Watson that a smile is the result of a sweetly working duct," I said to goad him. "The Isles of Langerhans are man's true paradise."

Freud bit off the end of a fresh cigar. It was a symbolic gesture, and I understood it as such.

I showed him the scars the lion had given me, but he only laughed.

"Each of us has his lion ready to rend him with its sharp claws."

The lion may have been illusory, but the scars were real!

He went on to suggest that reality is nothing more than an accidental form the energy of the cosmos assumes from one moment to the next. Only this, he declared, could account for the fundamental instability of matter. "Avalanche, flood, earthquake, drought—all register the agitation of what Charcot called 'the world's unconscious mind.'"

For Freud, nature is—by nature—hysterical.

8:00 P.M.

The Invisible Man sat down at the bar next to us.

Freud pronounced on him thus: "What you see on that bar stool is a manifestation of Wells' desire for anonymity. His terrible need for privacy has created an alter ego. But his alter ego's invisibility is in conflict with Wells' exhibitionism. Thus we have before us the curious paradox of an invisible man in evening clothes."

This was, of course, utter nonsense. Wells was in Mombasa, hoping to seduce Mrs. Willoughby; a shameless voyeur, the Invisible Man followed him, hoping to watch.

I watched him pour a whiskey into the void between his bandaged chin and nose. I listened to him smack his invisible lips.

"I will be happy to treat your split personality, H. G.," said Freud, leaning across me to hand the Invisible Man his card.

"He isn't Wells!" I said through gritted teeth.

Freud smiled patronizingly. (I was his patient, too.)

I clenched my fists, wanting to hit him. Displacing my aggression as I had been taught, I abused my body instead—my heart and other of the internal organs.

Sousa and his troop of players struck up a march.

I hate marches and complained bitterly to the bartender, who whispered something into Sousa's ear.

Sousa tapped the music stand with his swizzle stick (*baton*, I mean) and launched into a waltz ("The Tennessee" or "The Missouri").

I invited the Invisible Man to dance.

He accepted graciously.

"One, two, three…one, two, three," I counted as we waltzed awkwardly around the barroom.

Freud shook his head in disapproval.

"You are relapsing," he cried.

I gestured rudely at him.

"You must have therapy at once!" he shouted. "Before it's too late!"

I hugged the Invisible Man closer, and we danced in a little circle in the center of the room.

Freud began to sob at the destruction of the transference and of the minute linkages by which I had been, until that moment, attached (however tenuously) to normality.

In spite, I continued to dance with the Invisible Man. As we lurched about the floor (neither of us could waltz worth a damn!), his bandages began to unravel. During the playing of the second waltz ("The Missouri" or "The Tennessee"), I tripped.

And fell on my face.

"You see how dangerous it is to cherish an illusion!" Freud shouted in the midst of his weeping.

I laughed hysterically.

(I leave a little white space here in which to rest my nerves a while.)

After a while.

I broke with Fraud—I mean *Freud*! From now on, I was determined to embrace my neuroses. They were mine, and I would henceforth love them as I loved any other part of me (except my feet, which are flat, and my hair, which is gone).

"You have no self!" Freud screamed from the balcony of his office on Queen Victoria Street.

I did not give him the satisfaction of looking up. (I appeared to be talking to myself but was, in fact, in conversation with the Invisible Man, who was naked, because of the heat.)

November 4, 1918.

Wilfred Owen arrived, his lips corroded with the poetry of death. I am on my way, he said. Where? I asked. He smiled enigmatically, drank a glass of barley wine to fortify himself, and was gone.

November 11.

Armistice. The war fell silent at last; I did not have to listen to it anymore. I listened to Cole Porter instead, who was on his way home from the Foreign Legion. He had stopped at the Mombasa Hotel Bar and was singing about love. Mrs. Willoughby accompanied him on the piano. We smoked a cigarette together. Later, he eloped into the African night with the hatcheck girl. Those of us who were left never recovered our hats. *C'est la vie*! we said cheerfully, because of the armistice and because our imaginations were excited by thoughts of the hatcheck girl, with whom many of us had lain down in dreams.

1921.

Arthur Godfrey arrived with red hair and the white bell-bottoms and blouse of a sailor. I had my fortune told by a soothsayer in Constantinople, he said. I will become a famous radio and TV personality but will behave foolishly on the air, he said. I will die without regaining the love of the American people.

"What is TV?" I asked.

He didn't know.

1925.

Hemingway came, his hands smoking with blood.

"I am moving the feast to Mombasa," he said. "Paris is played out."

Gertrude Stein came, looking for Tender Buttons.

"A white hunter is nearly crazy," she said.

Next came Picasso, hunting for a Minotaur to take back to his studio.

(I had not seen one though I had heard its fierce bellowing.)

James Joyce came and tapped about the street with his cane in search of epiphanies.

(I knew of many such but decided against sharing them, for I was writing my own book.)

A Strange Period in which Time Delaminates.

And others came also! Jules Verne, for instance, in a hot-air balloon.

(He was dead, of course, but what did it matter?)

Darwin, also dead, came—and left, preferring the British Museum now that he could no longer be aroused by the sight of a naked woman.

Who else? The Shropshire Lad—he came, longing to be one and twenty once more.

(He was welcome to it!)

Did I mention the Wright brothers—Orville and Wilbur? They came to dream a new arithmetic of flight. And Klee wanted color color color, and Ziegfeld wanted women, and De Beers wanted diamonds, and Kurtz wanted ivory, and Tarzan wanted Jane, and the man who wrote Arrow Collar advertisements wanted literature, and the hatcheck girl wanted a honeymoon, and

the Titanic

swanned down

Queen Victoria Street

on its way to

the iceberg

(Believe me, I could do nothing to prevent it! It had happened
years before!)

They came—one and all—to pass before my eyes.

"They have no existence apart from your mind," Freud said,
who had crept into my room and tied me to the four posts of the
bed. "None of them is real—not even Mrs. Willoughby."

The beautiful lady was sleeping soundly next to me.

He lit a candle and, in spite of himself, watched with envy the
lascivious light.

"Touch her, Sigmund!" I whispered. (I would have touched her—
gladly!—but my hands were tied.) "Feel whether she is real or not!"

But he would not touch her, afraid that the strength of my desire
should have made her palpable.

"You are mad," he said, and then he struck me because he had
failed to convince me of it.

He opened a black leather-bound book and intoned, "Release—
oh, Agni!—this person who, bound and well secured, jabbers in the
toils of madness."

He pronounced the words backwards, then blew out the candle.

The Possible End of a History.

The Invisible Man has stalked me all down the century. He loves me, he says. He has shown me his nakedness, he says—his undisguised self. He cannot forget the moment when I took him in my arms in the Mombasa Hotel Bar and danced.

"Dance with me again!" the Invisible Man cries.

"I am too old to dance," I tell him.

I would rather sit and remember Mrs. Willoughby: how her hair tumbled down around her when I drew out the long pins; how she would step out of her white dress that lay at her feet like crumpled moonlight; and how, when Freud left the room after my ineffectual exorcism, she laughed and laughed.

"Dance with me!" the Invisible Man cries.

"Maybe tomorrow," I tell him.

He knows that I am lying.

"Why can't you love me?" he asks.

Angry, I rise up and feel around in the seemingly empty air in order to throttle him; but I cannot find him. (It is not easy to throttle an Invisible Man!)

"You are nothing!" he says to repay me for the hurt I have done him.

"You are nothing," says Freud, stepping out from behind the drapery.

"What are you doing here?" I ask in disbelief, because of the many years that have passed since last I saw him.

"I am with you always," he says with annoying familiarity.

"Come with me!" cries the Invisible Man.

"Come with me!" exhorts Freud. "Into the light of reason! The happy land of good mental health!"

The Invisible Man has put on a record: a song which, until that moment, never existed.

I look at the bed and see Mrs. Willoughby there. She raises her white arms, wanting to embrace me; and the sheet falls away from her breasts. I am aroused as of old.

"You never possessed her," Freud says. "One cannot possess what has never been."

"Liar!" I shout.

"You have lived your life among ghosts."

"Liar!" I shout again while I murder him. Apparently he has forgotten how dangerous it is to challenge a delusion.

Freud dies and, having died, disappears.

Mrs. Willoughby slowly disappears until there is only the tumbled down sheet to prove she was here with me. (Or was it I who tumbled it?)

The light stops mysteriously at the window; the room grows dark.

"I am what you have always longed to be," the Invisible Man says. "I am what you have become."

I fire my revolver at the sound of his voice. I listen to the bullet thud, the body fall to the floor. I light the lamp and watch as the corpse sprawls into the visible world again. As if only in death are we to be seen, finally, as we are.

Strange, that he should smile so.

CALLING THE ELEPHANTS

I had come to the end. The proscenium arch framed the wilderness, elaborating an idea of order among the mimosa. Darkness lay all about me—a soot. I put out my hand and was happy to see it steady. My anxiety had left me in Mombasa, in Mrs. Willoughby's arms. I would not see her again. I was done with all that, with the white arms of women and their unpinned hair...their lips. Done with bodies writhing or at rest. And also with gin: I had drunk my last weeks before, before setting out on the elephant paths that led irresistibly into the heart. A stirrup cup of the Queen's own for courage—then the plunge into night. I was not afraid here, where jungle birds rasp against silence. A silence minutely veined with whispers. Darkness smote me, but my courage stuck. I had come to the end of dreaming and had nothing more to fear from night.

I lounged against the stage apron. The gas-jets hissed. Stiff and greenish, their light thrust into the clearing, disturbing the atoms of primordial night, momentarily confusing them until, having recovered their ancient authority, they pushed back the light, threatening to swamp the footlights and occlude the heart itself.

You say: I do not understand what you mean by a stage.

A stage—such as one would find in a music hall or vaudeville house. Made of wood, with a heavy, somewhat threadbare curtain, equipped with painted backdrops, embellished with decorative molding, fretwork, masks of tragedy and comedy, a smirking cupid meant to insinuate lust.

You say: I do not understand how a stage should come to be in the middle of the jungle—in the heart of Africa.

Why not?

You ask: Who built it?

It was built or it materialized....

You ask: For what purpose?

I think it means that here will be enacted ultimate mysteries. The invisible, made visible. A minstrelsy of physical law—a burlesque show where all is finally revealed.

You say: I think you must be crazy!

(Yes. But sober and chaste.)

Jane stepped out of the foliage. She was dressed in jungle *dishabille*; the sight of her thighs and breasts teased with garish light tested my resolve. I reached for my pocket flask when I remembered having given it to the porter as a parting gift.

To Ali. For Good and Faithful Service.

"Jane!" I said, surprised, for I had believed myself alone at the center of a labyrinth and of a darkness altogether personal.

She put her hand on my arm. I patted it to comfort her, for I could see that she was distressed.

"I can't find Tarzan," she said. "He went into the trees yesterday and never returned."

I glanced at the stage as if the mystery of Tarzan's absence might be explained there, but the stage was empty.

You ask: About those painted backdrops...?

What about them?

You say: I should like to know what they represent.

They are scenery.

You say: But what do they depict?

Scenes of my past.

You ask: Your recent past—in Africa?

Yes, and earlier—a child in Cincinnati rolling a hoop that spun gold in the summer light...a boy in Cincinnati watching the boats steam up the Ohio...a young man in Cincinnati climbing dark stairs towards the body of a woman, feeling desire uncoiling in him like a watch-spring.

You laugh: It is not so easy to forget!

(I have dragged the past with me like the heavy apparatus of a magic-lantern show. Memory sticks to me like a burr!)

"He is full of doubts," Jane said with a tremor in her voice.

I was astonished! I thought Tarzan the most self-possessed of men.

"He worries how posterity will judge him. He wishes to make a contribution—"

"His is to preserve the wildness in the species, lest we become effete."

In this he was the opposite of Prince Kong, a swaggering beast set on becoming a man. Cruel lips, yellow spats, and gloves!

"I read him a newspaper account of the building of the Panama Canal. He cursed himself as a seeker after sensation, an idler, and hedonist. He cut his long hair and wept for his empty life."

I was sorry for him. Tarzan had always been, for me, an antidote to the over-refinements of Mombasa. When I had had my fill of Freud and Caruso, fancy dress balls at the Mombasa Club and Mrs. Willoughby's *soirées*, I would run into the jungle to be with Tarzan. There we would spend delightful days in monosyllabic conversation and, in the afternoon, spy on Jane bathing at the waterfall. (A Susanna in her bath.)

"How did you find me, Jane?"

"You left a trail of broken images."

I touched her.

"You are no dream," I said.

"You have come to the end of dreaming."

How did she know!

"You must help me find Tarzan!" Jane pleaded.

I was reluctant to leave the place I had reached with so much difficulty. It was restful—the end of dreaming. The empty stage waiting for revelations. The prettily sketched scenery drawn from memory. The whispering dark. The cessation of all confusions and uncertainties. I might have lounged there for an age, lighting my cigars at the gas-jet, studying the ash. Fortunately, I had with me several boxes of cigars. (Having forsworn women and liquor, I must have some pleasure!)

"Please!"

I looked at her heart-shaped face and imagined covering it with kisses. (Yes, yes—I had renounced desire! But that was in the absence of women. It is quite a different story when a woman is in the vicinity—especially one as pleasant to look at as Jane.)

She put her hand on my arm and appealed to me mutely with her eyes.

I sighed—for her, for the flame drawing up through the narrow ducts of desire, and for the loss of tranquility.

"Lead on, Jane; I will follow you."

To return from the end of dreaming took no more effort than the closing of our eyes. We fell into something like a swoon and in an instant were transported to the edge of consciousness.

You ask (with the air of a prosecutor exulting over an inconsistency in an accused's testimony): *Whose* consciousness?

But this time I will not answer you, having grown impatient with your fatuous quibbles.

We fell into a swoon—Jane and I—and arrived at the edge of consciousness and, opening our eyes, saw a mist behind which, or in which, were barely discernible shapes. Like one of Whistler's nocturnes.

You pronounce: I do not like them, or any of the spotted daubings of the Impressionists, who dally with light and immateriality. What we want from our artists is a clear definition of substance, lacking as it is in our lives at the beginning of the twentieth century.

Sick to death at last of my interlocutor, I raise my double-barreled Holland and send him *posthaste* into another dimension.

The transubstantiating mist cleared.

"Where are we?" asked Jane, befuddled momentarily by the speed of our flight.

"Where all things are possible," I replied self-consciously, knowing that I might well sound foolish to anyone other than myself (an aspect of whom I'd just blasted). "In an ellipsis, tucked inside time and space such as that Einstein and I had safaried once in Africa."

"I don't understand," she said.

I dibbled the dust with my finger, thrice:

. . .

"A seam in the world—in the world's *mind*—between History and the Imagination," I said solemnly.

She looked at me without comprehension.

I shrugged; I could say no more.

"But where is Tarzan?" she cried.

Tarzan sat in a mope. In his freshly shorn hair and morning coat, yellow vest and striped trousers, he reminded me of Oscar Wilde. I did not think his tonsorial and sartorial transformation became him.

Jane hurried across the clearing and embraced him.

"Tarzan, darling!" she murmured. "Where have you been, my love?"

(Oh, how I envied him—the big galoot!)

"I've been to Mombasa," he said. "I took elocution and dancing lessons. I lived in a hotel and bathed twice a day in a tub with feet. I hoped to become a gentleman."

He took a cigar case from his pocket and offered me a Partagas. He selected one for himself and sniffed cautiously its entire length in an amazingly fastidious manner, his handsome nose wrinkling and snuffling at the brown wrapper; and with this primitive gesture, his new gentility fell away, and the brute I adored was revealed.

It must have cheered Jane, too, for she threw her arms around his neck again and nibbled at his ear.

"Why did you return to the jungle?" I asked him, for it was the jungle in which we stood and beamed—Jane and I; Tarzan did not beam. He sulked.

"I did not fit into Mombasa society," he said ruefully. "I committed one *gaucherie* after another. At the Mombasa Club, I got drunk and called the elephants."

He beat his yellow-vested breast and—well, I have not the verb to render his uncouth yawp.

"And did the elephants come?" I asked.

"Oh, they always come," Tarzan answered, and I could not decide whether it was a boast or a regret.

"Always," Jane nodded in agreement.

"They were very hard on the carpets," he said, giving me a look as if I were somehow to blame. (I assure you that I was not!)

"Poor, Tarzan!" she said, petting him.

"I was expelled from the club for life."

Tarzan bowed his head and would have wept openly had he not been Tarzan.

"The majordomo told me I am no gentleman."

"I know the majordomo and he's a finicky bastard," I said.

"I was taken into custody and released into the care of Dr. Freud."

Siggie never misses an opportunity to enlarge his understanding of dementia. Tarzan's atavism is certainly worth a monograph.

"The elephants got away," he continued, more cheerfully.

Tarzan had found Freud's Queen Victoria Street consulting room confining. Having had the pleasure of that couch, I agree that the little room can be stifling, especially after Sigmund has been smoking. Then a heavy blue cloud fills it, nuzzling the grotesque wallpaper flowers with their gigantic, obscenely lolling stamens. Do you like my wallpaper? he invariably will ask me. I detest it but dare not confess it, or he will look over the tops of his glasses at me as if in triumph at this latest proof of man's fear of sex. Tarzan escaped psychoanalysis by the window, over the rooftops, and into the jungle, which opened to receive him.

"I'm glad about the elephants," I said.

"What do we do now," Tarzan asked, "to escape the boredom of an empty life?"

I suggested a musical evening.

"And tomorrow?" he said, his voice betraying profound anxiety. (How well I know it!)

I shrugged. I could do nothing to lessen the terror of the way ahead: the endless hours that will be his, until a mauling or bullet stop him short. Life will bring its sorrows; he will endure them or not. Life will offer up its solaces: Jane will tousle his hair (grown long again) and look at him as if there were no other man on earth, until she elopes with an archaeologist or a De Beers man. Later, Boy will console Tarzan for having been born, until Boy leaves or raises his hand to smite him. There was nothing I could do for the once King of the Jungle now that he had come to consciousness.

"Better you had stayed the happy ape man," I told him. Insouciant and careless of the weight of each impending moment—how they weigh down and defeat us all!

He looked down at his vest, then smiled at me.

"There are compensations, I suppose..." he said shyly. "For being civilized."

He liked that yellow vest!

I put a record on the gramophone, cranked it, and waited for the music to crackle into life. (It did—it always does!) Tarzan took Jane in his arms, and they danced on the silvered grass. (There was a moon and stars, for this was not the end of dreaming.) I sat on a camp stool, lit my Partagas, and allowed myself to drift. Hand in hand, Tarzan and Jane ran into the trees. I remembered what Ross had said, long ago, as the comet punctuated the night with cold fire:

"Thank you, my friends, for this dream!"

It is not craven to love the magical night! To love women and long for the arabesques of laughter and desire! I have hunted for death and almost found it. Tomorrow I shall go to Mombasa and buy a yellow vest. I shall find myself a lovely girl to be alone with in the trees.

I stood up and mounted the small hill on the edge of the clearing and, throwing back my head, I called to the elephants.

The elephants trumpeted in answer.

Life is an illusion. The illusion, however, is terribly attractive.